Warehouse

M S Green
Alan Green
Clayton Devanny
Simon Nodder
Jono Bell

Editor: Ian Daley

route

First Published in 2002 by Route
School Lane, Glasshoughton, West Yorks, WF10 4QH
e-mail: books@route-online.com

ISBN: 1 901927 10 5

Cover Design: Andy Campbell
Cover Images: Kevin Reynolds and Dean Smith

Editor: Ian Daley

Thanks to
M Y Alam, Carmen Blanquez, Anthony Cropper, Isabel Daley,
James Gilligan, Roger Green, Lorna Hey, Harry Malkin,
and everyone else who has helped along the way.

Printed by Bookmarque Ltd, Croydon, Surrey

CD duplication by Clipstore of Leeds.

Full details of the Route programme of books
can be found on our website
www.route-online.com

Route is the fiction imprint of YAC, a registered charity No 1007443

YAC is supported by
Yorkshire Arts, Wakefield MDC, West Yorkshire Grants

Introduction

'People who see their lives as a shipwreck set out to hunt down the guilty parties.' – Milan Kundera, *Ignorance*

The *Warehouse* collection is a series of linked short stories with musical accompaniment that is inspired by, and in some cases driven by, a very specific urban subculture. It is drawn from aspects of life that are rarely exposed and created by a group who are seldom afforded artistic expression. The words and sounds sit together to form the whole picture. The subject matter is at times harsh and uncomfortable. However, if you are able to slide beneath the surface and avoid any prejudice, you will discover a richness of expression that is breathlessly universal. This is a story of how life forms itself around given conditions and could easily be transferred to many places around the world. This introduction's intent is to provide you with a brief resume of the necessary context for the people and the place.

The majority of contributors to this collection, either as writer or musician, have at some time plied their trade as a warehouse operative. The exceptions being one who works in a factory, and one who operates a till on the check-out. They all inhabit the very compact urban conurbation that flanks the A1/M1/M62 interchange just south of Leeds; most of the action in the book takes place in one small town. Visitors to the town will comment on its character, even its prettiness, they will also notice the surrounding industrial landscape, dominated by the eight giant cooling towers of a nearby power station.

The town itself boasts centuries of history. Standing midway between London and Edinburgh, Edward I referred to it as the 'Key to the North'. This strategic positioning has dictated its fate. The Romans set-up camp around a huge signalling beacon; the Normans constructed an imposing castle and set up a stronghold. During its day, the castle had a reputation for being particularly bloody, it was also reported that it would fire cannon intermittently onto the townsfolk to keep them quiet. Following a long and painful siege during the Civil War, the locals requested Cromwell's permission to pull the castle down, and it was granted. The castle that took centuries to build was down within weeks and much of the town was rebuilt using its stone.

The coal industry and the supporting mining culture have dominated the area for the last century, up until recently when, following a yearlong strike, the majority of pits were closed down. The remaining wash of cheap labour and the good road networks attracted multi-national corporations with distribution centres, their warehouses soon becoming the economic lifeblood of the area.

That was then, this is now. For those employed at the lower end of the labour market, the once protective arm of the trade union has given way. Instead of job security, sick pay and annual holidays, insecurity and short term contracts are all that are on offer. The mining culture, once almost communist, has also moved on, connected as it is to environmental circumstance and the modern society through the expanding reach of the media.

The traditional route into a warehouse job is through temporary-employment agencies that contract on a day-to-day basis and for an hourly rate much lower than the company employees who the temps would be working alongside. If you show dedication, hard work and flexibility, there is a chance you won't be laid off at the end of the busy season. The work is mind-numbing, repetitive and physical. Often temporary employees work as long as they can stand or until they have earned the money they set out to, then they will rest for a while before re-emerging somewhere else.

The day life of a warehouse operative basically involves unloading suppliers lorries and transferring their content to designated sections of the warehouse, and also picking individual items from the warehouse floor and loading them on to a lorry which will then dispatch them to the retailer. Day in, day out. This is an arterial function of the economy; the book you are holding has already passed through at least three separate warehouses.

For a lot of the young men, work is seen as a necessary evil in order to fund an active social life. Premium lager is the order of the day, Stella Artois if available. Jack Daniels is the standard chaser. Drum is the tobacco of choice and is readily available at black market prices. Blue cigarette papers are obligatory, usually Rizla. The dope is strictly grow-your-own, always bud, strains of which come with names like AK47 and PR1.

Of other drugs, acid and mushrooms are not uncommon, pills for certain events are *de rigueur*. Cocaine is present and welcome, but not that often. And then there is the very real prospect of a heroin problem if you are not careful, and many aren't. One of the numerous housing estates in the area was recognised as having the largest per-capita heroin problem in the UK.

A big night-out could entail a trip to Leeds, but mainly it is local, the town was recently known to hold more pubs per square mile than anywhere else in England. There is one, discretely tucked away in a corner, that is well known for its unfashionable décor and its very strong lager. Any session that starts there will generally turn into a mammoth one. A session is not without its hazards, gangs of men from surrounding towns tour the bars in packs wearing their very local identity with pride and are prepared to fight for it. Bouncers are the first line of authority and they do not pull their punches. The loud and dark nightclubs are traditional hunting grounds for one-night stands, and the local park an established venue for casual sex.

This collection has been slowly drawn together over a four-year period, the music on the CD is the soundtrack for this time. *The Chapter* provides warehouse blues, music for late night candle-lit melancholy and metaphor. (The story that follows these songs around is that they were composed on top of a stack of fridges, on nightshift.) *Budists'* dirty urban funk supplies the energy and readiness that all young men possess. A number of the stories featured in the book are based on real events, which from time to time have been topics of conversation, accompanied by other gossip far too salacious to be written down here. As a whole, these stories and this music take you right to the heart of the matter.

There is no claim that the people who have contributed to this collection are totally representative of the norm, far from it. These people are filled with creative spirit, are giants within the community and, in part at least, its ray of hope. If you are left wondering what life could be like in such a place, slide in your CD, read on, and enjoy it in all its glory and splendour.

Ian Daley

Supermarket

Crude crass somehow slick slow-fast - that popartastic place where supply meets demand. You can reach out and touch...mouth-watering packets and tins...aisle after aisle after aisle...a little something that every household needs.

Created on production lines that won't - not ever - stop: brought to you by the all-conquering army...the cash toting cigar smoking econometric New Order. Wearing suit and tie and polished shoes too. Gulp! May the market force be with you.

And yes. Aisle after aisle after aisle.

Gimmicky glamorously precision placed panoramically.

Regiments and battalions of product.

A military profit parade.

Nation-wide, in every branch in every town, enough strategy and logistics to go to the war. The price war. Never-ending tit-for-tat and junk mail shots. 'They got 3p off a loaf we got 4p off pasta 6p off spreads supreme saving blasta. Collect coupons for mystery gift too.' Relentless loaded jingle rhymes...technicolor zany...acme deadly...yes, lip-shot-rounds-propaganda-for-pounds targeted straight between the eyes. A hit is all that matters. And the aim is seldom untrue. For Machiavellian shrink types have probed the collective housewife psyche and this their monstrous masterpiece - a sly surveyed spectre of the donkey and carrot. All out attack on all fronts - a fanfare of ballyhoo, soundbites, consumer rights. Promotions. Quality means goods that do not come back for customers that do. Your statutory rights are not affected in the event that you - the treasured customer - voice any complaint. Worth your weight in chicken nuggets.

People power, spending power.

Mothers of low income families. Rebellious, hopeless or couldn't-care-less at school, minds now as arith+metic+ulous as a top-of-the-range multi purpose calculator. Instantly registering when the budget is stretched to the limit; though sometimes spluttering when the cerebral batteries are in need of a recharge, worn down by howling tots. Today, on checkout five, the usually perfectly gauged load is over and the red-faced mother returns the most extravagant item to the shelves. The more affluent lady behind tuts at the time wasting and is thankful the shame is not hers. Lady Affluent compares the contents of her trolley with that of Mrs Poor. Double or treble the amount, bigger and better names, more sweets and treats, a slab of steak rather than a tin of Spam. A wry smile appears on the lips of the Lady. She will not have to struggle to the taxi-rank or bus depot but instead ride home in the four wheel drive Land Cruiser in the car park. The Lady is exalted, the glory of savoir vivre. Status justly exemplified by tins. A trolley-load of tins. And all because this Lady loved the right man.

Aged ad catch-phrases remembered easier than the Rights Of Man. Liberty, equality, for mash get Smash. Fraternity and fart fertile food.

Eat work eat sleep. Eat work eat sleep. Eat work eat sleep. Eat work eat sleep. Repeat. Existence like a receipt off the roll. Lucky horses, lucky teams, lucky numbers. The big one. Life is a lottery, for many a no-win fruit machine. Get your hands in your purses and pockets. Feed the machine. Videos, CDs, paperbacks, garden tools, garbage. Cartoon magnets, painkillers, insect repellent, sun lotion.

Bikini-clad cardboard cut-outs present the latest got-to-have goods. Sponsored soaps. Commercials starring idealised actors. The image is the message. The message a blur and flurry of spiritual sucker-punches. Strangely subtle as the punch-drunk populace race and rush to get on with the rest of their lives.

Born mortal into credit infinite.

Mass media culture society. Buy in bulk, it's cheap and sexy, sleazy too. Cheapo mega-pack fish fingers - 'sounds like foreplay with a whore' thought a sex-hungry single young male aloud. The blue-rinse pensioner beside him goldfished her shock and disapproval. No matter, there is a pet section. Dog food, toys, hamster cages, birdseed and stuff for pussies, naturally. Recently recognised, in some poll or other, as the nation's favourite pet. Until the next poll. Financed by X brand dog food. In the magazine section, as a new line, filed under 'Men's Interest', girlie mags are flogged. Wrapped and concealed in black-blot-out polythene. Putting the time-honoured alleyway newsagent out of business.

Sex sells and no-one is surprised. Never have been. It is the world's oldest profession, after all. Still, much ear-scratching and intellectual gender debate. Money-makers pay lip service to libertarianism, prudish pseuds question the ethics and wisdom. The world looks on, as if there could have been any other winner.

'££££££££££££'
'££££££££££££££'
'££££££££££££££'

Money talks. Big business and its little brother big jargon. They sold you...Coca-Cola, Pepsi-Cola, lemonade, lime 'n' soda. MacCleans, Colgate, Aquafresh. Scrub the sugary rot of capitalism away. New improved formula approved by the revolutionary British Dental Association. Comrades in arms, fighting the decay-dant oppressor plaque.

Meet the new boss.

Going Back There

Outside, the pitch-dark chill of a November's night swept across the countryside. Branches of dimly silhouetted trees swayed and contorted like limb shadows of grotesque ballerinas - a sinister performance that whipped in and out of vision as the train shuttled purposefully along the tracks. Destination drawing ever closer. Occasionally, when cloud cover broke, a moonlit meadow slipped by. Waters of summertime's still-life ponds tumultuously rippled and whirled. Dilapidated barn doors moodily slammed closed and open, creaking groaning remonstrations unheard beneath the desolate indifference of winter's withering breath. The wind that, out here, seemed only to grow in power and savagery.

Surely the train would soon leave the hills and fields behind, trundle through the concrete sprawl of a town the traveller would at least partly recognise, be able to put a name to.

A feeling of foreboding - one that had simmered and stewed for weeks now - rose within the man. Many yesterdays - lost now found, hidden, rediscovered, familiar - crashed with cruel clarity to the fore of conscious. He shuddered; and he fought back.

The past is over and done with. Dead and buried. They should have left the past alone, to rest in peace. I've waited too long for the past to forgive and be forgotten. Now this.

The man wished that he had journeyed by car. Imagined the relief and ease with which he spun the steering and the vehicle skidding into a U-turn, racing away. Away from...because he couldn't face it, didn't feel strong enough to. Of course he couldn't really turn back, he knew

17

that. Something deep inside had been disturbed, revived. Some heartfelt longing that for years had lain dormant was now awake, hungry, compelled, with a will of its own. The sensation - whatever it was - threatened to eat him away, from the insides out, if not satisfied.

The train's quick. More comfortable than such a distance by car. I prefer train.

The traveller sat at one end of a carriage, travelling in the opposite direction to that he faced. Hurtling backwards...as ever.

There were two other passengers. One, a middle-aged businessman, was seated centrally: his mouth agape releasing gentle snores synchronised to the rhythm of the rails. A shiny leather briefcase was placed on the seat beside him, a folded broadsheet rested tidily in his lap. The other passenger, a young brunette dressed sensibly in brown, sat reading from a tatty paperback at the opposite end of the carriage. One leg was crossed protectively over the other. The girl's light make-up highlighted a pretty yet unremarkable face; one of those people who look remotely familiar and yet are irritatingly impossible to place. As if she might resemble a comparatively famous actress, the type that have secondary roles in serialised thrillers.

The traveller's wristwatch had stopped at seven thirty. Irrationally he searched for significance...how? why? could it?...nothing to be found, nothing other than his own jitters. He ran hand through hair and ground teeth. Significance, symbols - all day long he had been looking out for them. Like a crazy fool might.

The businessman snored on, it was the end of a long day. The traveller knew that he too needed sleep. But not here; he wouldn't sleep here.

Every so often, chance intervals, the female passenger would covertly glance up, uneasy about being alone on a train at this time of night. First she would check on the businessman, see that he was still in the land of nod. Then she would check on the traveller, her eyes darting nervously back to the pages of her novel whenever a suspicion of contact was established. The traveller considered her aversion a small mercy. Contact was something he too was eager to avoid.

I was a waste: my mind roamed, my body fidgeted...ever since the letter...

Dear David, So glad we've finally managed to find you. If only you knew how hard we've tried to get in touch. We all hope that you're well. Over the last few years things have changed so much for the better. Mother has improved immensely - she has even returned to work, all of four years ago now. The same type of stuff, office work. She worries about you. Dad's much the same as before - before the accident, that is. Everybody says so.

Joanne and I have missed you more than words can say. There's so much I want to say. I've never been much good at expressing my feelings by letter - we need to talk. Really need to talk.

Joanne is to be married in a few weeks. Would you? Could you? Come. It would make everybody so happy. We all would love to see you again.

Please write or phone.

All the love in the world,

Alexis.

PS Sorry the letter's so short but I really am hopeless with them. It would be so much easier to talk. And much better. We need to talk. Please come.

There was also a wedding invitation, signed with love from Joanne. And that was it. The first communication in over a decade...

Another train, speeding from where this one was heading. There was a whooshing sound, an amplification of the rat-at-tat-tat rattling of the tracks. Both the traveller and the young woman peered into the lighted carriages of the other train. A few indistinct faces peered back. In a matter of seconds nobody was there.

I had read the letter after returning to the flat from work. Pouring over the contents five, six, seven times I slumped, stupefied, on the edge of the bed. Stared into space. Thoughts scrambled, an eternity seemed to pass. Numbed. As if spirit had vacated body, abandoned this plain for another...a twilight zone where past, present, future ceased to exist. A realm where, through fractured instances pulsed streams of random experience. Entwined, twisted sketches of life - my life - becoming dreams within dreams. Psyche an unwilling audience to a scarring subliminal slide-show. I'd suffered flashbacks before but this...

The businessman seemed to yawn in his sleep, as if his dreams were dull, prosaic.

Eventually something jolted me out of the daze, perhaps the slamming of a car door as a neighbour arrived home eager to flee indoors. I noticed that the living room was freezing cold. My fingers fumbled to light the gas fire, trembled to stir sugar in the brew I made. I put the envelope, letter and invitation to the bottom of a junk-filled drawer and tried to dismiss them. Live for now not then. We were each other's pasts, nothing more. So I had believed. It was hopeless. On the Thursday night of the same week, having got drunk on cheap red wine and after three days of emotional turmoil, I wrote back. My reply even briefer than the letter Alexis had posted. Amongst other things, I supposed it better than her turning up on the doorstep unannounced.

Dear Alex,
In answer to your letter - yes, I will come. Please send me the details.

I posted the letter that same night. It was raining heavily. Only when the letter had dropped to the bottom of the post-box did I realise that I'd failed to sign my name. In the morning, no longer under the influence of alcohol, I regretted putting pen to paper at all.

A ticket inspector appeared in the doorway of the carriage farthest from the engine; he casually glanced up and down, checking that he had checked everyone's tickets. The inspector's eyes settled on the woman who had begun rummaging through her bag, looking for her ticket. Looking up, ticket between thumb and forefinger, she found that the ticket inspector had walked. The businessman had not stirred. The traveller had not seen, his eyes were vacant, someplace else...

Alexis was swift; within days I received my sister's response. Apparently the family were all over the moon, Mother especially. My parents would put me up, in my old room. Don't worry they'd love to, Alexis wrote, they all couldn't wait to see me. I wish I could say that the feeling was reciprocated.

Regardless, I had all but arrived. Home. To attend the wedding of my long-lost sister, Joanne. My intentionally long-lost sister.

There had been four kids. Alexis the youngest, Joanne two years her elder, me, two years older still, and the first-born, John. Eleven months separated us brothers.

My brother.
John.

The swing-a-cat yards of a row of terraces; the gutted remains of a derelict windmill; a steel bridge that vibrated and whined under the bulk of the train as it carried the few people inside safely over the gloomy depths of an inky black river. Dense vegetation; open countryside: on a faraway vista the street lamps of a hamlet or village twinkled as if the stars had fallen from the blank heavens above to smoulder on the earth below.

Drizzle began to fleck the windows.

I still saw my brother, intermittently. His visits were peaceful now, unlike before...He would always come after midnight, still barely a teenager, dressed exactly as the day it happened. The same blue and white hooped T-shirt, faded patched jeans and scuffed playing out trainers. Brown hair tousled as if he had just been wrestling, an infectious cheeky grin exposing two buck teeth. He left the brace out, always hated the brace. With palms open, fingers outstretched, my brother would slowly but confidently amble toward me. 'We're still friends, David. It doesn't really matter.' A gentle whisper that somehow sang out like a congregational hymn; sparing, healing. John would pause a couple of yards from me, stand grinning, carefree. In seconds - maybe hours - the image would disintegrate. Into ashes, fine dust. I'd notice that the echo of the sweet gospel melody had also diminished, away, away, into silence. Nothing but sleep followed.

I would awake refreshed, serene. Strangely serene. It hadn't always been like this.

Go away.

The businessman came to, puffy eyed and disorientated. Blinking around, realising his whereabouts, he flashed an embarrassed smile in the traveller's direction, checked over his shoulder at the woman behind. Then he collected his paper, flicked through pages and - a suitably interesting headline. Throat cleared with a dry cough, a final glance - this time with a cool air of aloof distinction - and the businessman commenced to read.

From the corner of her eye the woman looked both men over. Finally reassured that propriety had not been compromised she dived back into the pages of her book.

I sank into a stark past nightmare...Down...Into a keeling revolving room of scarlet walls. Round and round and danger. My brother stumbling and twisting and screaming. Claustrophobic terror. His legs mechanised, arms

21

restricted by a bile stained straitjacket. He wanted out. Out. To Get Out! A camera lens view. The camera zooms in. Close. Closer. A gruesome facial shot. A retching geyser of offal, of gore...the ravaged socket where the right eye once...should have been. Hideously disfigured, my goofy clown brother adorned in a costume of filth. The circus is not in town. Ha! Ha! Ha! Closer. Come closer. Howling and wailing. Thrashing. And the dagger sharp fangs. Possessed. A monster. Of whose creation? I hear my father's voice, 'David!' I want to respond...the scene warps...flips...confusion...out of focus...clearer...a happy freeze-frame of school chums; the pirouetting flamenco of mother's musical jewellery box; a tartan scarf; the chiming collection of clocks - its time! The Pipkins?!...orbiting back...wide arcs...collapsing...from within...from within talons pierce and tear through the cloth of the madhouse overcoat, ripping it from around John. Shed like reptile skin. The flesh beneath rife with oversized lice, gorging on gaping rotting stinking wounds. Blood froths on swollen lips. The child's lips. The blood on the walls of the room. I don't want to look, see this! The horror of the damned. With the beast's talons John stabs, mutilates, mangles, mauls, his own decomposing neck. Savagely severing head from shoulders. The intact eye - the left eye - manic. Frantic. Ferocious. Round and round and faster. Blurring, dizzying, nauseating. Stop! The zombie offers the decapitation as if a gruesome prize. 'You did it! You did it!' The dripping mouth and its voodoo chant. Of truth or lies?

Back on the train the traveller squeezed his eyes tight.

Push it all out.

The businessman, the young woman, did not notice anything.

And years ago...terrified, delirious, I would bury my head in the pillow and sob wretchedly, unsure whether I was asleep or awake. Nightfall was the dread of my whole angst scourged early teens. At the foot of my bed, for hours at a time, I often prayed.

Fumbling in his pocket, producing a coin, the traveller started to push back the cuticles from over his nails. An occupation.

But it wouldn't go away.

My mother suffered a series of violent breakdowns. My father became a distant ashen-faced stranger, a completely different character to the fun-loving prankster we had all loved. Friends drifted out of my life. I was no fun to be with. 'You ruined everything!' Joanne, the elder of my sisters, would spitefully wail, her arms punching out vengeful and wild as she exorcised her own anguish whenever we were alone together. I didn't strike back, instead cowered away, into the corners. Waiting for the beatings to cease. They didn't hurt. Physically.

The businessman smiled, a little private smile. Reaching into the inside pocket of his suit jacket he took out a pen. The crossword.

My grandparents hadn't quite known how to react. Whenever they were around things became unbearably uncomfortable, not that life was much easier when they weren't around. The family seniors would sombrely shuffle into our living room, nod grave discreet greetings and then be seated. Waiting. Someone was always waiting. In itself their reticence would have been an ordeal, had my dad not cleared his throat and stiffly requested, 'David, out to play in the garden, will you?' My sisters stayed indoors, went to their room.

The businessman thoughtfully chewed the end of his pen. The woman turned a page.

Of my grandparents there was no mention in Alexis' second correspondence. Maybe they had passed on.

'Observation; scrutiny. Twelve letters. Begins with S.' The businessman spoke his thoughts aloud. The woman looked up, frowning.

I had counselling. Dr Alice Brady, a gentle and kind-mannered lady, probably in her forties back then. She was of little help, though she did try. I simply hated any form of questioning, it wasn't anybody else's business. I wanted to lock it all in, throw away the key. And so for the duration of the sessions I would remain stubbornly mute. By now I'd started playing truant from school and it wasn't long before my absenteeism extended to Dr Brady's chats, as she described them. My dad, eyes constantly darkened by lack of sleep and worry, decreed that I didn't have to go if I didn't want to. It was what I'd wanted to hear.

Of the family, only little Alexis didn't outcast me. With the passage of time, the knowledge it brings, I'm not even sure that the others did so. Maybe I outcast myself. I liked solitude for certain. My infant sister would stand patiently in the doorway to my - and what had been John's - bedroom, fully aware that I knew she was there, ignoring her. Suddenly baby Alexis would rush in, throw her arms tenderly around me. 'I don't blame you. I don't blame you. It wasn't your fault. I don't blame you,' she would mournfully cry. It felt like everyone else blamed me. You could say I had a lonely childhood.

The train was slowing as the traveller stood, made his way to the toilet. He tried reviving himself, splashed his face with cold water. His mind had started with the games. The traveller's mind is full of tricks and games, and especially when fatigued or stressed.

In the mirror, behind me, he was there. Seen too many movies - I always tell myself that whenever I see ghosts.

The traveller read the warning : NO SMOKING. MAXIMUM PENALTY £50. The traveller risked £50.

The train stopped as I extinguished my cigarette under the tap. It pulled away as I reclaimed my seat. I didn't catch the name of the station. I couldn't identify any of the surrounding town either. Not that it appeared memorable in anyway.

Still didn't know how far to the journey's end.

My fellow passengers had disembarked. Their departure worsened my loneliness, my alienation. As much as I didn't want to talk I didn't want to be entirely alone. Not now.

I had left home at seventeen - couldn't stand the atmosphere a moment longer. More a convenient means of escape rather than any ambition that lead me to uniform, the army. 'Guns,' my father had said, sour and disappointed and as much to the dishes he was washing up as to anyone. That was all anybody said on the matter. They had more important issues to contend with.

The traveller squashed the cigarette under his foot. Coughed.

Mother had had another relapse. She was still on the psychiatric ward when I left for the training camp. I didn't visit her, didn't say good-bye. Everything about my departure was low-key, dry-eyed. I thought they were all glad to see the back of me.

All those years ago, youthful but far from untainted, I looked back as the taxi gathered speed. The curtains were pulled to one side. It hadn't been possible to make out who stood in the window. 'Burn some rubber, my man,' I implored the driver. The relief was that of a prisoner of war on liberation day. It was best for everyone concerned.

The train rattled.

By then even Alexis didn't have much time for me. But she did have first kisses, homework and an insane mother to cope with. That's trouble enough for any hormone flooded girl without having to suffer the mood swings of a churlish, withdrawn brother.

And then there was what had happened to John.

24

Dad wrote a couple of times, Alexis the once. I hardly bothered to read the letters, let alone reply.

Opening the small bag of luggage beside him the traveller took out a bottle of orange, put the drink to his lips. Zipping the holdall closed he contemplated another cigarette - only three left in the packet. He'd need them for later. He rued not buying a newspaper, looked over hoping that the businessman had left his; no. The weight of his eyelids told him he was probably too tired to read anyway. But he needed focus. He wanted to stop thinking.

I never shot anyone in the army. Didn't do all that much in the army. Got pissed in the NAAFI, slept with my quota of soldier sloppy dames...and read. Mountains and mountains of books - out of my craving for seclusion rather than any desire to better the education I'd missed out on. Sure, I went on the obligatory tours - was verbally abused by the Catholics in Belfast, got a suntan in Cyprus - but sooner, rather than later, I realised I was unsuited to the lifestyle. The discipline I grew to hate. By my twenty-second birthday I was on civvy street once more; without direction. Renting a rundown dowdy flat over a newsagents in Kings Cross I stumbled into labouring on building sites. At weekends I'd roam the neighbourhood's bars, then those of the city, drinking heavily, provoking stupid fights with strangers. Soon, with a reputation as a troublemaker, I flitted to another part of London, tried to quieten down, took a job selling tickets in a cinema. Stacked shelves in an hypermarket, became a car park attendant. Whatever I undertook to pay the bills I soon bored, moved onto something else: they were all positions without prospects. Didn't know how to settle. Couldn't stay in one house - forever hiring vans, changing my address. Girlfriends came and went, not one of them lasting more than a few months. Not one of them forming a lasting impression. I was unlovable, they were unlovable - or else the relationships were simply convenient arrangements for sex. Then I stopped meeting girls altogether, released myself by visiting hookers. It was no big deal.

I became one of those fallen, bitter men who prop up bars, slurring; philosophising that luck is everything, life continual flips of the same coin. Heads or tails? Like a curse the coin always landed on the wrong side...I continued to drift...days, weeks, then months, seasons...years slipped by.

Going nowhere.

Then, two years ago, came the change. The miracle. John visited me in the night, for the first time that merciful and peaceful cherub - no longer the agonised little fiend, maiming itself, wanting to hurt. It was a revelation. Immediately I vowed to improve my lot. There were difficulties getting a better job - but I was persistent - finally I wormed my way into the ranks of a large stationery firm, was granted a company car, pension, began work as a sales rep. It was easy to talk about things so meaningless and dull as pens, paper, formatted disks. I set about hunting down more pleasant, respectable - though still sparsely modest - accommodation. There I've stayed ever since.

My love life never improved.

And then, then there was the letter. Considering the intense restlessness, my non-stop moving, it's hardly surprising my family had such trouble locating me. I'm thirty now, years on a bleak winding road behind me, scrawled on my CV. Sat sleepless and agitated on that train-on-straight-tracks only God knew what lie ahead.

The train had slipped into the very heart of provincialdom. Town after town. The cooling towers of a Power Station loomed massive, grimy but resolutely proud, upright over the miniature block buildings beneath. Then glimmers, half-flashes - sightings that gave the traveller something back. A shop front, a bus stop ten yards from an old stone bridge, pubs by cross-roads, a housing estate that somehow, viewed at this particular angle from the rail-line, stood out from all the similar rest. Just commonplace things. Black and white photos in a box in the attic.

God only knew how Alexis found me in a tiny maisonette in Streatham. She'll be twenty-six by now. A young woman. Was she married? And my parents, Joanne...

Nearly there.

I closed my eyes. Coaxed myself; told myself to relax. Listened to the metallic lullaby of wheels on tracks. They lived at the same address. Everything would be better when everybody was reconciled, relax. Exhaustion worsened the nervousness, the anxiety. Take it easy. Take it in your stride.

Had the traveller's eyes been open he would have recognised the confectionery factory that the engine and carriages now passed.

'David! David!' Hearing my brother's excitement I turned and watched him leap down the steps that led to and from the rear of the house. He was wearing his favourite white and blue hooped T-shirt...IT WOULD BE BETTER IF

YOU WOKE UP...John's face shone with pride, his buck teeth revealed; he was even wearing the brace, obviously trying to please Mother. He paraded the reason in his hands. A brand new air-rifle.

'Dad's finally got me one. It's an early birthday present.'

I scowled. I was jealous. John sensed that straightaway. He knew me only too well. 'Don't worry,' he said, 'you can use it too. I'll let you. As long as you promise to be careful. It's really powerful - a .22. You can have my best catapult too. Here, hold it if you like.' John was always generous to me...WAKE UP DAVID, YOU KNOW WHAT COMES NEXT...I weighed the gun in my hands, invigorated by a feeling of power; a boy dreaming of manhood. I peered down the sights pretending that I was a soldier of fortune, the pigeon perched on the roof gutter, a sworn enemy. 'It's a real beauty,' I enthused to John. We grinned at each other. We'd wanted an air-gun for ages. 'I can't believe it!'

'I couldn't when Dad gave it to me.'

Why? I still don't really know. That universal tomfoolery of young boys? I redirected the barrel of the gun so that it aimed point-blank in John's face. We were no more than two yards apart. FOR CHRIST'S SAKE WAKE UP! YOU'RE NEARLY HOME! 'Halt, who goes there? Friend or foe?'

'Don't pull the trigger it's...' **BANG!**

I jolted upright. My fringe, as usual, matted to brow. The nape of my neck soaked like I'd neglected to towel dry it after taking a bath. Though I had scant time to worry about any of that. I'd arrived. Home. The train had eased into the station as I slept. Rattled, ragged, I grabbed my belongings and scrambled to the exit, reaching it just in time. The guard was about to motion to the driver.

The train became smaller and smaller until it disappeared altogether around a bend in the line. Only then did the traveller wipe the moisture from his forehead.

The warning had come too late. I was a kid, excited, my finger had innocently squeezed the trigger. The pellet tore through the eye and entered the brain. Killing John instantly. How was I to know the safety catch was off? How was I to know the gun was loaded? Perhaps John had been too young to have a gun. They should have...

It's no good apportioning blame. Too late for that. It's all in the past, over and done with. Dead and buried. My dad was just being the same old generous dad he'd always been. Dad and John had both been full of generosity.

The station was unmanned, deserted. No one else had left the train.

His legs felt weak, as if they couldn't go on.

Only the advertisements appeared to have changed since he'd left, thirteen years ago. A beauty suggestively putting a chocolate bar to her mouth. Beside her a poster proclaimed 'there is always a Samaritan in this station'. A picture of a telephone. A number. 'Running away won't solve anything', another notice read in bold black letters.

An owl hooted from somewhere high in the nearby trees. The hairs of my neck stood: I half expected John to materialise in front of me. Of course he didn't. He was dead.

The gale had abated, though the sky was still laden with cloud. It would rain soon.

I pulled myself together. Told myself to think positive. This was it. I started walking.

Alexis had wrote that I should phone her as soon as I arrived, she was going to pick me up. But not just yet. I was hungry. I needed to curb my apprehension too. I decided to head into town, find a Kebab shop that was still serving. It wouldn't yet be eleven o'clock. The train had been scheduled to arrive at twenty to.

The street outside was also deserted, bar a solitary parked car. The headlights blinked on as the traveller stepped out onto the pavement, almost blinding him. He heard the car door open, close, then a voice. 'David?'

This was it.

I hadn't meant to do it John, you knew that, didn't you?

'Alexis?'

The person started running towards him.

Inside the Devil's Lungs

I remember the day all the weight of Hell was lifted from my shoulders, the day the Devil decided not to fight me any more. I was called into the manager's office to be given the news that my services would no longer be required in the warehouse, I was being laid off. There was part of me that was worried about how I was going to be able to live, after all, you need money to live, but there was part of me that was so relieved and when I balanced out the worries and the relief, I realised everything would be alright. A weight had gone, the weight of Hell itself, a weight so immense that it could have pushed me through the Earth's crust and dug me into the deepest, tightest hole of all.

It's strange that Hell is so close to Heaven. There you are in a heavenly slumber, in the warmth of your bed dreaming how life could be, then your alarm starts screaming at you to wake up and go to Hell. You get into your uniform, you've time for breakfast then it's off to the bus station.

'One to Hell please' you say to the bus driver.

You're on the 189 from Leeds to Wakefield and five minutes you're there, Hell.

Whitwood Industrial Estate.

I remember when I first started working in the warehouse, I started on the same day as John. John was a bit of a lad, considered himself to be a bit rebellious with his shagging around and heavy drinking, but he looked and acted exactly the same as everyone else in that godforsaken hellhole. He was just like all the other slaves. I was so different, none of that well-groomed look, no 'decent' haircut and cleanly shaven chin, not for me, oh no, I was ridiculed for my hippy hair and heavy stubble, my beads and my yellow tinted glasses freaked 'em right out. I could see on their faces a 'What the fuck have we got here?' look right from the first time they saw me. I became known as the Yeti, a new age traveller and even Jesus Christ himself. I was never going to conform to their ideals, no way.

John fitted in right from the start, no pisstaking for him, unlike me.

I could see strange things about the whole place, things nobody else could see, maybe it was my yellow tinted glasses that gave me the ability to see. The manager was the same bloke I'd had as a manager at a thousand other warehouses, a skinny little fella, immaculately shaven, lightly greased hair combed back. He wore a tie showing his support for the local cricket team, he never smoked or got drunk. His wardrobe consisted of hundreds of white shirts and black trousers, always in exactly the same style. Strange that I'd seen this manager a thousand times in a thousand different guises because I can remember somebody once saying that Satan has a thousand faces.

The material of the warehouse, the bricks and mortar, looked too organic for me, like being inside the lungs of a giant beast. I saw many a man having their soul smoked, big drags from the beast inhaling every last molecule of the addictive narcotic which ruled the beast's existence. I saw it happening, their eyes would slowly turn an empty, gray colour as the lifeforce within was soaked up into the spongy lining of the beast's lungs. These people were too easily tempted by shift bonuses and overtime. Money, money, money, the root of all evil. All these people cared about was money, the temptation was too much. John never noticed his soul screaming for salvation because all he saw was the money rolling in.

The Devil tried tempting me with love but you can't love or be loved by someone who is causing you harm. I'd felt true love before so I noticed the Devil's trickery. I knew this wasn't love because it burned me with the intensity of Hellfire and left me charred. I got myself out of that relationship.

True love had bleached blonde hair and real inner pains. Love soothed those pains, an unconditional healing process. The Devil destroys everything, almost, I can't be with my true love but that love will live forever, both inside me and inside her.

The shift supervisor came over to me and told me I was wanted in the manager's office. I knew what was coming, relief. The devil had given up on fighting me, I was too strong.

'I'm sorry to tell you...' he started '...but we'll not be renewing your contract.' Marvellous!!

With those words I knew I was being given freedom.

The last night I was there I left the building at the end of the shift and I felt so sorry for those lost souls I was leaving behind. As I walked outside I was greeted by a heavenly sight. The most beautiful sunrise I'd ever seen illuminated the sky, the clouds were amazingly dense and red, like Mars, floating in our atmosphere. The clouds spoke, welcomed me to heaven. The sky was warm and full of life. It was time for me to rise.

I felt a tingling sensation in my back as my wings unfolded. I was an angel. I turned into vapour as I flew upwards, towards the rising sun. The true love inside me swelled and exploded like some beautiful firework and scattered across the world. I was to become love itself.

My final human thoughts before turning into pure emotion were an exorcism for the souls of the warehouse operatives I'd left behind.

'I exorcise thee O impious Satan. In vain dost thou boast of this deed. I command thee to restore it as a proof before the whole world that when God receiveth a sinner, thou hast no longer any rule over his soul. I abjure thee, by him who expelled thee from thy stronghold, bereft thee of the arms which thou didst trust in, and distributed thy spoils. Return therefore this deed whereby this creature of God foolishly bound himself to thy service; return it, I say in His name by whom thy art overcome. When thy power has come to nothing, presume not longer to retain this useless document. By penitence already hath this creature of God restored himself to his true lord, spurning thy yoke, hoping in the Devine mercy for defence against thine assaults.'

Supermarket

Derek Saddleby. A man with the pleasurable personality, if not quite the ambition, of any number of historical despots. He patrols the gangways of groceries. With the single-mindedness of a KGB super sleuth examines each stack of tinned beans, carrots, peas. The compartments of refrigerators and freezers are all, bar none, subject to his icy tyrannical gaze. To Saddleby's chagrin frozen parsnips are slightly under-stocked. Teeth grind, chin juts out and the first unfortunate shelf-stacker the manager spies is ordered, humiliatingly in front of staring spectators, to the managerial office.

'I will not tolerate shoddy work. Do you understand?' At the end of a lengthy lecture exonerating the virtues of hard graft Saddleby's mush is beetroot red.

'The frozen veg were not my responsibility this week.'

Saddleby's eyes bulge, his moustache twitches and his cheeks blaze a bloodier shade than the skin of Beelzebub himself. Not so pretty in perdition pink. And devilry manifests itself in different forms to different people, it seems. The shelf-stacker cannot help but think that Saddleby resembles a bloke in a photo in an unreturned school textbook. Only Saddleby has a crazed look opposed to the calm of the bloke in the photo. Jo Trotsky-or-something-to-do-with-starlings the bloke was called. The bloke in the photo had a fuller head of hair as well.

Stalin Saddleby cannot help but notice the shelf-stacker's faraway gaze. Ever more outraged the manager slams a paperweight hard against his desktop and the shelf-stacker, a cherub-faced school leaver working for little more than peanuts, jumps nervously. Saddleby's breathing is irregular. Eventually his voice, a snakelike hiss, whips on words: 'this is a team game. Team. T-E-A-M. Do you comprehend, idiot?'

The youth's eyes sheen with saltwater, he swallows and swallows the choking lump of apple in his throat. The induction to harsh reality is never easy. Good-bye playground, hello big bad world. 'I've only got one pair of hands.' The boy's voice is a tiny tremor.

'What! You insolent mutinous brat.' There can be no doubt that the manager is some sort of demon. Just look at that chameleon complexion - from hammer and sickle red to swastika black, darker than the skies of Good Friday, the day the Jew got nailed. Today is also the thirteenth. 'Out. Get out. Your P45 will be in the post. Insubordination will bring the whole enterprise down in ruins. Complain to head office! Knock down the walls of Citizens Advice! Insubordination has got to be trampled underfoot...'

'Dogshit, that's the only thing you'll trample underfoot.' The boy, amazed at his own outburst - his squeezing of the verbal trigger - departs faster than a defector who scaled the Berlin wall. Saddleby's hands ruffle his thinning wig. 'God, they don't make them like they used to,' he complains. If only he could get them from Siberia. They'd be cheap from Auschwitz, too. Bah! Minimum wage?

Derek Saddleby takes his position very seriously. He is a man avoided and thought little of by the rank and file below him. The disliked manager will sometimes dine in the supermarket cafe to rub shoulders with those-who-pay-his-salary-and-the-plebs'-wages, as he sees it. Keeping in touch with the fickle source of cash flow; a swing-o-meter for enhanced service. Nosy bastard. Snooping Saddleby is all ears to the public's private conversations while the cook and the waitress look on, discussing ways of slipping arsenic into his meal. Playfully of course, but as the women themselves say, if they could get away with it...

Derek Saddleby; after shaving early on a morn gazes in the bathroom mirror and swells with pride. The receding hairline, the ever deepening, multiplying wrinkles, the drooping and puffed features - signs of youth waning further and deeper into a murky past as the weak, weakening flesh approaches it's fifty second birthday. Except Sir Derek sees none of this. Instead, there, before him, the reflection of a morally upright gentleman of maturity. A stiff upper-lipped patriot and proud. The very backbone of society. An imperial cliche, and irrefutably modern all the same. As Saddleby flicks through the filofax of his mind he pauses, deliberates, then smiles. He would be a martyr to the cause. At the high altar - the Chamber of Commerce - he would gladly offer himself as a sacrifice. Providing he got a mention in the Queen's honours list.

We all have a dream.

Married to the still pretty Deborah Saddleby with two teenage daughters, Elizabeth and Victoria. On Acacia Avenue the family castle is entrenched. A three bedroomed semi with a medium sized garden in a middle-class estate in the suburbs. Patio, ornamental facade and that subconscious uniformity of well trimmed lawn and conifers. Essential particulars to an unsung hero of the rat race.

Nothing spectacular, middle and medium some sort of achievement. Moderation, the theme of this morning's brief discourse with Fitzgerald James an estate agent from across the street. Like identical reflections in the same shop window both men nod a respectful farewell, climb into their cars, spark the ignition and away, away to work. Dek, as he was known in the school yard of his formative years amidst a scruffy mining community, is a social snob. Prejudice well demonstrated by his reading of *The Daily Mail* - which he has left behind at home - and his public posing with *The Times* - which is placed on the vacant passenger seat. His own father used to have the *Mirror* delivered. Saddleby loathes the fact that the store he manages stocks that bolshy braggart's bible. He is, of course, embarrassed by his dad's trade union links.

Derek Saddleby, a Dr Jekyll and Mr Hyde. In scorching summertime, banqueting on a back garden barbecue, he declares marriage and family life to be sacred institutions. 'Nothing, but nothing, should come before family.' After casting a chicken drum bone into the bin Saddleby emphasises his point by clapping loudly and rubbing together greasy hands. The neighbours, freeloading on lager, smile peaceably over the garden fence. While the other guests sigh intimately as Derek pecks his wife on the cheek and hugs each of his blushing daughters.

Hours later Deborah is fast asleep on the couch having downed one too many white wines. Derek's princesses are upstairs risking paternal disownment by puffing on king-sized joints of pot. And the man of the house takes his chance, surreptitiously visiting a website of sexual contacts on the computer in the study, adjacent to the kitchen. Friendly neighbourhood family man Saddleby chomps on a pork and pickle sandwich while despatching his favourite fantasies and fetishes down the phone line: 'Oh Whiplash Wendy I lurve you honey!'

Every other Monday Derek visits a buxom masseur in Leeds. He comes home late hiding behind the pretence that he has had to attend important business meetings with regional reps and company top brass. On late closings, 8:30pm Tuesday and Thursday, Saddleby locks up and visits the nearby Squash club to unwind with like-minded associates. Over a short or two the business brotherhood lust after the breasty barmaids. 'Haw-haw-haw-haw,' they all sycophantically snort at one another's terrible jokes until closing time.

There are telltale signs that somehow Mr Derek has completely, remarkably, unintelligibly missed. On home's answering machine the plumber's voice is also that of an electrician. Is also a member of Deborah's non-existent reading group. Is also the mythical Mrs Gilbert's son, wondering where on earth his mother could be. There is the red rose that never withers on Deborah's bedside table. And the sudden appearance of socks of a pattern or colour that Saddleby would never have chosen. 'Oh, I bought you those for Christmas, don't you remember?' Derek is not sure that he does, but he does not want to appear ungrateful.

Should the fellow inhabitants of Acacia Avenue have less an eye for the material and more an eye for the personal it would be no great feat of observation to note that Mrs Deborah Saddleby has been having an affair with a toy-boy nineteen years her junior for over twenty months.

The wild-child daughters are out with mates and dates, at the youth club or in the pub, the virtuous parents know not. The illicit lovers are entwined in bed having just made passionate love for the third frantic time that evening. On the chest of drawers there is a photograph of a pot-bellied man shading his eyes from a blistering sun and wearing a preposterously out-of-vogue pair of swimming trunks. Together the seductress and the satyr laugh at the image. The older woman strokes the hairs of the young stud's chest, kisses him slowly on the neck, then teases her fingers across a gym-shaped hip and thigh until her hand gently caresses the crotch. The young stud quietly groans, turns his head and nibbles the older woman's earlobe. 'Whatever possessed you to marry such a prat in the first place?' He whispers huskily. The other man's wife kisses her muscular plaything again, giggles and murmurs, 'we all do something we regret when we're younger. But he was different back then.' Then upbeat, expectantly, cheekily, 'do you think you can rise to the occasion again?'

'I think I could be persuaded.' Still giggling Deborah slides away, repositions herself on the bed and takes the young stud in her mouth.

Sex sells and no-one is surprised. It is the only thing Deborah Saddleby has left, trapped as she is, in a loveless marriage with an uninteresting prig. Perhaps it would be pig if Deborah knew what a big knockered masseur-cum-whore was doing right now for one hundred and fifty pounds. Derek has gone for the full works this week.

Squelch

So there I was again in the shift manager's office. I was looking at the same safety at work posters and his tacky Porsche calendar wondering if he suffered from a penis envy complex whilst trying to look solemn, apologetic and vaguely interested in the shite he was saying.

'We need more effort on your time keeping Alan and at least some interest in the overtime we are offering because it's all reviewed and taken into account when we consider renewing your contract.' He said.

Not fucking likely I thought and tried to think of something convincing and reassuring to tell him. But it was Friday, pay day, I was going to Leeds that evening, and thoughts and scenarios of the night ahead were distracting me, working as a mental cushion to the bullshit I was having to listen to. I made some shallow excuses to him, looked enthusiastic about what had been said but I knew deep down that he'd heard it all a million times before, and that this was probably just part of some sick and twisted mind game that he enjoyed playing. He then dismissed me, like a Gestapo commandant. The temptation to do a Nazi salute was overpowering, but I showed enormous self control and walked out of the office with a grin on my face shaking my head thinking 'what a wanker'. I then wondered if he was sat at his desk shaking his head thinking the same.

I left his office at the same moment his secretary was selecting papers from a filing cabinet. She was nice to say the least and as I walked past I caught the waft of her perfume and femininity. I grabbed the opportunity, with both hands, to quickly look at her arse and deliciously pert tits. Lurid thoughts manifested, but disappeared as I entered the warehouse. I tried to switch off and get into my work but admittedly was failing miserably.

At this point Pete and Steve, arguably the company's most full on, solid, never a day off or late workers approached wanting to know what had or hadn't been said in the office earlier. They were obviously delighting in the fact that in the company's eyes they were the golden boys who set the example, and were never in the office themselves for anything more than to talk and chat about company expansion, and the possibility of working weekends. So there was me, undoubtedly the finest fuck-up the company had ever employed, having opinions that mean nothing to me, forced upon me by the golden boys when I couldn't really give two fucks about them or their lifestyle. Instead of making moral judgements on my beliefs and ridiculing them, they should be trying to understand, that's how I look at it anyway, each to their own.

They seemed incredulous to the fact that I wasn't too interested in owning a car on finance or getting a first time buyers mortgage or working my precious weekends on the whim of a manager or supervisor, and that the things that are important to me need a lot less effort than overtime. Spending quality time with my daughter and watching her smile, smoking in parks on sunny days, being creased over with laughter in the company of a few select friends. Even walking the dog on a mild morning, these things seem infinitely more important to me than anything the work place can offer. The weekly wage is nice, but to me is not essential. There are more important things in life. After listening to their drivel for ten minutes I felt drained. William Burroughs once wrote that if after meeting somebody you felt negative and drained, the best thing to do is avoid them. Good advice, but it's not always possible at work. I'd had enough by this time so I spent the last half hour before dinner sat on the toilet lid reading last week's *Sport* and adding to the graffiti on the cubicle wall.

After dinner, time dragged along at a typically afternoon pace. It was probably slower for me due to the joint I'd had in the break, for medicinal purposes, and to try to re-align my karmic calmness. It had worked. I found it easier to float above the bullshit than to try and wade through it. The weed had taken the edge off life just nicely but it doesn't do much for motivation at work, which is probably why the supervisor came to see me twice about being behind with my work. I justified this by telling him that in not completing the tasks they had set me along with the other people who didn't finish, that this would lead to a backlog of jobs being incomplete. Thus leading to overtime and weekend work for my illustrious work colleagues who required it to support their new cars etc. Live and let live brother, I told him. I could tell he wasn't impressed but I didn't care. I was at the don't-give-a-fuck stage on a Friday afternoon. There was only an hour left of the shift, but isn't it funny how the last hour at work can drag on and seem to last for an eternity? And drag it did.

A nightmare bus journey ensued after work. The bus was packed, which left a fat woman, who stank, with no option but to sit next to me. Every time she shifted position or moved I caught an overpowering waft of her repugnant BO. Her two kids looked like street urchins from a Dickens novel and proceeded to play Power Rangers at twenty decibels, in the guise of Tasmanian devils. As the woman turned and tried making polite conversation, the whole situation on the bus started to get on top of, and then swamp me. I felt alienated and isolated from everyone on the bus. After a shift at work I didn't need this at all. They were just ordinary folk going about their business, but I had never classed myself or wanted to be accepted as ordinary. Individualistic is more appropriate.

It was almost claustrophobic now and although it meant walking I just had to get off. I rang the bell and squeezed myself to the front of the bus. The doors swung open and I stepped off. Breathing in a sigh of relief I almost choked on diesel fumes as the bus pulled away. I put my hands in my pockets and started walking, taking in the panoramic view of industrialisation, the power stations and chemical works, glass factories and the pit. Then I was on the Warwick estate. I walked past the local gypsies playing football hearing them shout 'MUSH, MUSH, TO RONNIE MUSH. QUICK MUSH, RONNIE, RONNIE, RONNIE. FUCKING HELL RONNIE WHY DINT YA GIVE IT BACK TO OUR MUSH' and couldn't help but laugh at the argument that followed.

I had a five minute chat to two friends who had succumbed to a healthy heroin addiction, which is hard to avoid on the estate, unless you have got your head screwed on. They looked yellow and thin and as though they were about to die. They had no front teeth due to the amount of tooting they had employed, but it's like I say, live and let live. Leaving them I walked down Grassmere, passing whole rows of graffiti covered, decrepit, boarded up houses and found it hard to believe that this country has a housing problem. Five minutes later I was home, running a bath and making something to eat.

Within the hour I was heading out of the door on my way to Leeds.

As I sat on the train it pulled away. I paid the conductor noticing that there were only three other people on the train. A middle-aged man reading some magazine, and a young lad and lass embracing, kissing passionately, making that clop clop clop sound that accompanies any heavy petting session. I gave it twenty minutes and spent the rest of the journey having a swift reefer in the toilet. When I stepped out of the cubicle, as the train pulled up to the station, the distinctive pungent aroma of cannabis filled the carriage. Accompanying it was a two-inch layer of thick smoke at ankle level which must have escaped through a small vent in the bottom of the toilet door. That's the only problem with skunk. It fucking reeks. The conductor who was stood at the open train doors couldn't have failed to notice or smell it. Instant paranoia gripped me as I was half expecting him to have the transport police waiting, but as I approached him as casually as I could, he just smiled and said 'smells nice'.

As soon as my feet hit the Leeds streets after the chaotic hustle and bustle of the train station, I was off. Bouncing, full of energy and excitement, strutting like John Travolta in *Saturday Night Fever*. My plan for the night was to have a couple of drinks somewhere chilled and then meet a couple of friends later. Calling to the cash point I drew a cheeky sixty quid out and smiled when I realised that there were more funds available if I needed them, which often happens. I made my way to *Arts Bar* entered and ordered a drink. I found a quiet corner and sat chilling contemplating how I had seen Leeds go through a complete metamorphosis from being a dirty post Victorian town, with derelict warehouses and its fair share of rough and ready taverns, into the vibrant, resurgent business capital of the north. Just goes to show how anything can change. It was at this point that she walked in. This girl looked fabulous, supermodelesque, totally unreachable and out of my class. She carried herself like a young bohemian. I wanted to marry her there and then. It took me another couple of drinks to think 'fuck it you never know until you try'. I walked over and bantered small talk before offering her a drink, which she accepted. She was totally approachable and seemed quite intellectual. I allowed myself, whilst stood at the bar ordering drinks, to entertain thoughts and daydreams of walking through parks with her hand in hand, on mild autumn days, kicking leaves, listening to her laughter but the bubbles around these thoughts abruptly burst a couple of minutes later when I offered to meet up a little later on. She explained that to spend any quality time with her would cost me around fifty quid an hour plus more for any extras. It explained why she was talking to me in the first place. After politely declining her offer, I left and headed to meet my mates.

It was around ten pm and the pill I had dropped was kicking in just nicely. I was enjoying the warm loving feeling along with everyone and everything, even the prick of a boss at work and the fat woman included, when an absolute babe walked through the door, with her mate. She was stunning and she smiled as she walked past. It was a welcomed distraction as my mate Jonny Boy was talking pissed up bullshit in my ear. I kept sneaking a peek at her and became convinced that she was throwing furtive glances in my direction. Or was it just me? With all the bravado and big headed confidence of someone who at the time believed himself to be the coolest person on the planet, I strolled nonchalantly over with the panache of Bond and the swagger of John Wayne. After polite introductions I found myself at the bar ordering three drinks, having been invited to join them. I was excited to say the least. The conversation flowed for a while and I was loving it. Paranoia kept taking hold as the waves of warmth fuelled by the alcohol and drugs washed over me, threatening to reduce me into a slavering, gibbering wreck, but I was handling the situation well. Her mate was making excuses, wanting them to leave. It's funny how the not so pretty ones find prior engagements when better looking friends start getting attention, but Miss Stunning said she was OK and wanted to hang around for a while which was an enormous ego boost. After a five minute debate and having convinced her friend that my intentions were honourable and that I wasn't a pipe wielding maniac, she left us. This was my opportunity, but first I had a more pressing matter. With the tea I'd eaten earlier mixed with the cocktail of liquor and class 'A's on top, I suddenly, and to my utmost horror, discovered that without even the slightest hint or warning, I needed the toilet. It was imperative, the situation was desperate. With all the airs and graces of Her Majesty, I politely excused myself and ushered myself to the gents. I was treading carefully as my mental faculties were swimming and slippery toilet floors have been the downfall of many an inebriant, but nevertheless I made it to the cubicle unscathed. I half stepped, half fell in and, with relief, locked the door and there was Mr Armitage Shanks. Pristine porcelain. Having dropped the appropriate attire, arse hit cold plastic. Mr Armitage Shanks must have been as out of it as I was because with one shift of the arse cheeks he pitched over dropping me sprawling to the floor.

With hindsight it's easy to see what happened. Mr Shanks needs four bolts to keep his base firmly secured to the floor but, for some unknown reason, someone somewhere decided this individual model needed only one. A slight shift in weight sent the whole toilet tipping over. Myself included. I was on the toilet floor, arms sprawled over the toilet pot, piss wet through from the water pipe that had burst, when *le WC* broke free from the floor, with my kegs round my ankles. I was now having what alcoholics refer to as a moment of clarity. I reached for the door handle to pull myself up with but my wet hand slipped and I was back on the floor. I managed to stand up and assess the damage done. Piss wet through and filthy from the floor, all I could think of was thank fuck for sanitation because it could have been worse, the toilet could have been full. My mind flashed back to the girl who was waiting, I quickly peeled off my top and gave it a quick rinse in the sink then smacked the hand dryer button. It didn't work. Fucking typical. I didn't relish the prospect of trying to explain what had just happened to a beautiful woman and no brilliant excuse came to mind. I opted for the only option open to me. With all the dignity and self-esteem that I could muster, I put my head down, left the toilets and headed directly for the door, making a peculiar squelching sound. I squelched down the street, procured a taxi, but the sadist who was driving said I had no chance in the state I was in. I squelched back to the train station, freezing by this time, still needing the toilet and coming down off the night rapidly. I bought a train ticket home with some sodden money that was only just accepted as legal tender and stood shivering on the platform waiting. I then caught the train home never to see little Miss Stunning again. I proceeded straight to the toilet badly needing it, and a spliff, only to discover that my weed was soaking too. BOLLOCKS!

Junk Food Mash

It's not that I claim to possess the prophetic power of John the Baptist when I say that I always knew Jamie would lose it, one day. If William Hill ran a book on such like a stake of a tenner would just about scrape winnings of a quid. It was that obvious. Yet, on an otherwise dreary run-of-the-mill Friday night, even I, Jamie's chief and probably only confidante at work, was shell-shocked by the hurricane blast towards oblivion...

We were in the employment of a shady and despicable local businessman, Mr Skankster, whose particular (or at least legitimate) forte was junk food. Cafes, burger vans, pizza palaces, fish 'n' chips shops - our illustrious paymaster had a grubby finger in every rancid out-of-date pie in the vicinity. Folklore has it that a Chinese restaurateur, armed with a deadly gigantic wok, once gave Skankster a slapstick yet hair-raising chase through the town's alleys and side streets after the venal wheeler and dealer had tried to introduce himself as a highly ranked member of the triads. This foolproof ploy, to steal a cut of Mr Chang's prospering enterprise, was hatched despite Skankster having as much oriental resemblance as a Yorkshire terrier. As ridiculous as it may seem, this anecdote underlines the brazen lengths - whether ludicrous, illegal or both - people believe our bossman was prepared to go to increase the swell of his wallet.

'Money mad and money to be made' would be Skankster's jovial, crocodile toothed parting shot to those ill-fated enough to meet him in the flesh. Naturally, as befits a man of such standing, wherever and whenever the wages of his minions were concerned, the budding

Colonel Sanders wasn't quite so enthusiastic when it came to placing greasy, grasping paws in bulging, bottomless pockets. Scrooge may well have redeemed himself after meeting the spirits of Christmas, but those selfsame spirits would be rushing woefully for the nearest bottle of meths should they cross the path of this damn cheapskate.

I was the fortunate one. I worked only one shift per week under Skankster's patronage - a few quid extra to boost the wages of a part-time bar job I'd taken whilst belatedly studying several college courses. Jamie, he was the unfortunate one. Six days every week, flattered with, but not by, the dubiously glorified title of 'special manager', he slaved in kitchens, over cafe counters, or as tonight, in a fast food mobile. All for an absurdly pitiful wad. Skankster's regular dogsbody-cum-doormat. So it goes without saying that Jamie despised the job, puked at the pay, and subsequently, for the first hour of work was as humanely spirited as a hardline Palestinian terrorist. With sly, gentle coercion these flames of resentment could gradually be doused and rancour would give way to casual chitchat. Of the loves of his life - football, films, shagging - he had an almost encyclopaedic knowledge. Minus the never-too-distant and deep-rooted frustration, which cut as deep as a mine shaft, Jamie could be an entertaining, likeable character. Providing he hadn't had a domestic with the wife earlier in the day.

That doomed Friday, having heard three furiously impatient emissions of a van's horn I'd hurried out into a chilly, wet November's night. Clambering into the passenger seat I immediately recognised that this shift would be especially burdensome. I could hardly fail to. 'Fucking skivvies to the world! Fuck all pay and fuck all say! Can you work this Sunday? Skankster's pile of shite food is entering my dreams and fuck knows what!' Flushed with belligerence Jamie flung a mobile phone onto the dashboard, crashed from reverse into second gear and the van shuddered on its journey. 'Erm...All right, Jamie?' Jamie glared through the windscreen onto the lamp lit road ahead, ignoring my greeting for perhaps twenty seconds before the spiralling taut ambience was shattered. 'All right, Jamie? Does it fucking look like it? Would I be driving this heap of crap if I was all right?'

'I suppose not.'

He drove with wanton abandon. Paying little attention to a pedestrian rushing home to escape the numbing, bitter cold the van aquaplaned around a corner, a foot slammed down on the pedal and the pedestrian was saturated. In the side view mirror the startled drowned rat gestured that the occupants of our vehicle were fond of playing with their genitals. 'Woah, we're not Starsky and Hutch. Slow down.'

'If that cunt, Skankster,' Jamie paused, almost choking on hate, 'ever asks me to work on Sunday again I'll wring his fucking neck.'

'I've told you before, just say no.'

'Just say no!' Jamie was incredulous. 'Have you ever tried telling Skankster you've better things to do. The fucker's got more whitewash than all the villas of the Mediterranean.'

Brakes were haphazardly applied as we approached a junction. Luckily I'd fastened my seat belt. Miraculously there was no other traffic. I massaged the stab of pain in my neck. 'For fuck's sake, cool it! You might want to be measured for a coffin tonight but I don't. OK?'

'I'm going to be cremated,' the driver muttered. With a sardonic smirk he jerked the van into forward motion once more.

Silence reigned for the remainder of our kamikaze ride into the abominable Mecca of boozy brawls and appalling musical taste - Pontefract town centre, the site of our pitch. Jamie, a shock of live wire nervous tension - agitatedly rocking his head from side to side, chewing on a lip, drumming fingers on the steering wheel. It didn't require an intellect of genius to fathom that something was seriously amiss. Gravely I looked into the black night above and prayed for heavenly intervention. The most devout atheist would want to believe in a blessed referee tonight.

My wristwatch read quarter-past eight. Burgers sizzled on the grill plate, hot dogs simmered in brine, pies warmed in the portable oven. Professional to a fault, Jamie cut, buttered and spat on the bread cakes. He'd probably tried to fertilise the mushy peas before picking me up.

The morbid silence went unbroken. We awaited the first punter. Bored. Ten minutes into the vigil I chipped at solid ice. 'Be quiet tonight. The weather's not fit to let a dog out and loads of people will be saving for Christmas.' No response.

The drizzle became a downpour. Raindrops mercilessly lashed against the weather worn pavement, forming little tributaries which flowed into grimy, flooding gutters. I scanned the whirlpools which had developed around a drain for evidence of someone else's luck. But a discarded rubber johnny did not materialise. A reflection peered vacantly back from a frozen food store.

'Been a bad week, then?' I reasoned that the storm inside the van must subside even if the one outside remained stubbornly offensive. Jamie picked his fingernails and yawned. 'Are you deaf?'

A glare.

'It's always a bad week, isn't it?'

'Come on. Get if off your chest. I'm not putting up with this all night.'

'You're not putting up with this all night! I put up with it all week! Fuck you!' His spite sent me reeling back a step, as if a blow had been struck.

'If that's the way you want it, have it. Fuck you as well.'

Pissed off by the rebuke, I leant against the counter, my attention once more drifting to the unspectacular world of rain. Uninviting shop fronts decorated with florescent card advertisements - discount prices on second rate goods. Dank, draughty doorways. A near desolate bus terminal swathed in a dim halo of artificial orange light. The No. 150 bus eased away, destination drunken nihility - or the loneliness or companionship within red-brick terraced homes. The bus was soon followed by a speeding taxi, perhaps heading to a pickup with a preened and perfumed reveller hungry for a night on the tiles. Thirty yards further down the road and hidden from view by the public transport depot the Post Office HQ forlornly stood. Its lights out and rooms deserted until the early hours whereupon sleepy-eyed workers would drag themselves disconsolately from their dreams, come to execute the mundane task of sorting giros, bills and letters from relatives and lovers. I wondered, did anyone send picture postcards from here?

I lit a cigarette. 'Don't smoke in the fucking van. It contravenes my health and hygiene standards. I'm your boss. Don't smoke in the fucking van.'

'Since when have you had hygiene standards?'

'Since right now.'

'I have a smoke every week.'

'You don't any longer.'

'Do you want me to walk? Twenty quid to put up with this! Do you want me to walk?'

Our eyes collided in a blitzkrieg, a blazing fusillade of vision.

'OK, OK. Smoke yourself to death. Why should I care? Set the van on fire if you want to. It doesn't matter to me.' This was no climb down. I anticipated another barbed swipe, only from a different vantage point. The cut and thrust was not long in coming. 'As it's so quiet tonight you might have to take a cut in wages. I might only be able to pay you fifteen quid.'

'Jamie, you either stop being a total twat or I'm going home. Twenty quid or...' I pointed in the direction of the bus station.

'Yeah, yeah.' A sneer flitted across my antagonist's features. 'I was only jesting. You'll get your twenty. Only winding you up.' An autistic infant would have known the threat had been humourless.

'Look,' a concession, a plea to good nature, 'whatever's eating you do something about it. You can't keep coming to work like this. Move forward. You're in a rut.'

'My wife's left me for another...' A hand suddenly shot upwards and clasped the mouth tight shut, as if angrily censoring it for blabbering the unspeakable. 'I'm over twenty five-years old,' Jamie continued after a minute's reflection, 'I work in a miserable low-paid job. I have no prospects. No social life. In a rut? I'm in a fucking mess.' A mess of gnashed teeth and eyes that glistened with the sad moisture of tears. His anguish froze my tongue, the enmity that had existed was paralysed. From nemesis to counsellor in the space of seconds I felt as if I held a useless dictionary, full of uncertain replies, meaningless wisdom.

'Sheeshburger, pleesh.' Never before had salvation arrived so heroically in the teetering image of a piss-artist. I assumed the cheery air of greasy Joe on a not so cheery evening. 'Onions with that?' A nod of confirmation. Two quid on the counter and a generous splattering of tomato ketchup. 'All day sesh! Home to bed,' the inebriated one explained. Wiping a glut of spilled sauce onto his shirt our premier customer staggered away, the epitome of a Hanna Barbera stooge that had received a hammer-strike to the head.

'You ought to see your doctor. Get a sick note for two weeks.' The drunk's perfectly timed interruption had provided breathing space to recover my bludgeoned wits. Jamie himself had gained an apparition of composure. 'Oh, I'm sorry, mate,' he apologised, placing a conciliatory mitt on my shoulder. 'I shouldn't be giving you all this grief. It's just, well, things have been getting on top of me.'

'They keep getting on top of you. We've had this conversation at least half-a-dozen times and the bottom line is you've got to get yourself another job to sort yourself out.'

'That's easier said than done. At least getting a job that won't drive me up the wall as much as this fucker does. I spend so much time gofering for Skankster I can't be tossed to search through papers when I get home. I haven't got time to wipe my arse most nights.'

'And the wife...has she really left?'

'For a twat who lives three streets away. She says I've neglected her. Says I spend too much time at work. The stupid bitch doesn't seem to realise it's all for her and the bairn. And what eats me the most is the fact that the slag's solution to our problems is to go and shag some dozy bastard from up the estate. I know I'm not the best of people to live with at the best of times but...'

'Where's Ronald McDonald when you need him?' Hell, was this some happy burger party tonight.

'Huh?'

'Nothing. Honestly.'

Jamie slung two chunks of flabby meat onto the stove, prodded them into the desired position with a breadknife. I opened the refrigerator. 'Have you started a distillery on the side?' Two litre bottles of Napoleon brandy lay prostrate on the top shelf. No wonder the sly devil had been so keen to get out the burgers and marg earlier.

'To get us through the night. Sixty hours every week in greasy kitchens, I deserve a drink now and again. Crack open a bottle now.

Put some coke in with it.'

'Are you sure drinking is a wise idea? You're not the most attractive drinking buddy on the planet, right now.'

'Pour a drink. Don't be such a queer.'

I resisted retorting that I would have rather been drinking with Dennis Nilson, instead poured two small measures into plastic beakers, adding a substantial quantity of coke.

'There's hardly any in there. Pass me the fucking bottle.' Jamie wrenched the brandy from my hands and took one long, lingering swig. 'That's what I call a drink,' he explained between coughs. He placed the bottle on a formica worktop from where I hastily collected it and stored it beneath the counter. 'If a copper walks by and sees that you can kiss good-bye to your driving licence.'

'Two hot dogs, please.' The make-up on the peroxide blond's face was way too heavy. Her friend, a brunette, huddled up, sharing the shelter of a garish pink umbrella. The brunette had the prettier face. Jamie served the pair. 'Couldn't get hot over you two dogs,' he observed curtly as he received their money.

'Cheeky cow, you're not exactly body beautiful,' the blond retaliated, part aggrieved, part marvelling at the audacity.

'Piss off.'

'Casanova could do with lessons from you when it comes to customer relations,' was all I could think to say. Jamie laughed.

It soon became clear that my sidekick was no heavy drinker. Two beakers and a large gulp to the bottle later and the lad visibly paraded signs of intoxication. The first indication, a jelly-legged lurch into the chassis of the van whilst reaching for a bottle of mustard. 'I'm not cleaning up any mess you create,' I joked. The alcohol had begun to play familiar and welcome tricks on me, too. Inhibitions, misgivings, vanishing like a marked card up a conjurer's sleeve. 'Don't get fucking clever.' A warning or deadpan banter? I wasn't sure.

For a brief period trade picked up. We worked in strained silence, except when vapidly communicating with the steady stream of weather beaten customers; a number of whom complained of the discourteous manner in which food was unceremoniously dumped before them. 'What do they expect?' Jamie snapped as the remnants of commercial success drifted away. 'It's not the bleeding Ritz. Expect me to be a Tom Cruise look-a-like with a fine line in gentlemanly flattery. Would Sir or Madame prefer the house wine? It tastes just like vinegar because it is vinegar, it's Aldi vintage and most rat-arsed pie and pea merchants recommend it.' I bit into my lower lip, savouring the shock of two obese middle-aged women who had stormed away, seething masses of outrage. Jamie had dictated to them the health benefits of slimming classes and Oil of Ulay.

'Is this the night with no end? What's the time?'

'Just gone ten.'

'What do you say? We'll call it a day and go back to my place and have a full blown session.'

'Skankster won't be pleased,' I tried to side-step the offer.

'Who cares what Skankster thinks?'

'You did, until you started knocking oversized measures of brandy down your neck.'

'Do you think I should knock the fuck out of the cunt who's pissed off with my wife?'

'I thought she'd pissed off with him.' I caught a full on glare but drink had lessened my ability to worry.

'Who pissed off with who has nothing to do with it. The twat has been jumping into my bed with my kid in the house. He deserves...' With his right hand Jamie mimed a throat slitting motion.

'I'd leave it. I honestly would. It won't solve anything and you'll only be walloped with a fine.'

'Whose side are you on? If I say he deserves a fucking kicking he deserves a fucking kicking.'

I shrugged, smiled. By now Mr Lovelorn wasn't the only soul with a fried mind. 'Have you ever seen that painting?'

'What the fuck's a painting got to do with anything?'

'That painting. The famous one.'

'Which fucking painting?'

'The Scream by...Who's it by?'

'Who gives a fuck?'

'Munch. Edvard Munch. The Scream. You remind me of that painting. Pure angst.'

'Are you taking the piss?' Jamie threateningly took a couple of steps towards me.

'No. No. Calm down. It's a work of art. You'd like it.'

'A work of art? I'd like it? My wife leaves me and you start comparing me to a fucking painting.' He slowly shook his head, complete and utter disbelief personified - the last mortal on earth capable of making any sense.

Right at that moment the mobile phone rang. Jamie lazily reached over the driver's seat. 'Twenty quid says it's Skankster checking up on his profits and all because I didn't lick his arse earlier.'

'Do I look so stupid I'd take a bet like that?'

'Hello, Mr Skankster (in mock joy)...Of course, everything is sweet and dandy, hunky-dory...Yes, I'm all right...Top of the bloody world...No, we haven't been drinking...Yes, I'm ever so sure...(a long break)...Who cares?...Anyway, me and Stevie reckon we deserve a few hours off, it's been a quiet night and we work ever so hard...It's a what you may call it? A revolution...(another long break)...In that case Mr Skankster, we'll be ever so happy to serve you one of your disgusting rotten burgers (snigger)...Mr Skankster, do you know what word rhymes with Skank?' The caller hung up. 'Pour me another one. It's time I had it out with Skankster.'

'He's coming here?'

'Yep.' I reached for the bottle of brandy. Without reservation. That swift one later two sunny Spain bleached babes stopped by. Full of drink, full of giggles, full of cleavage. 'Two cheeseburgers, please.'

'For two lovely ladies I'd do anything.'

'That's the worst start to a chat up line I've heard for months. You haven't got a complex about the size of your ding-dong, have you?' Much sisterly merriment. 'We read about it in magazines.'

'Now, now, ladies. A little decorum, please.'

'You look like James Bond...without a shag and before plastic surgery.'

Jamie ignored their laughter. 'Seeing that you're the most beautiful customers I've had the pleasure to satisfy all night, these are on the house.'

'What have you done to them?'

'As if. I only wish to show my appreciation of your head turning loveliness.'

They accepted the freebies with shrugs and perplexed, grudging gratitude. 'There's some weirdoes about,' the one with the longest legs was heard to comment as they headed in the direction of the nearest pub. Jamie wolf-whistled in their wake.

'What's got into you?'

'Liberation,' Jamie replied. The boy picked up a squeezy bottle of sauce, smirking evilly. Inspiration. A Pollockesque redecoration of the van commenced. Tomato ketchup, mustard, cheese slices spurted, plastered, slapped every which way, across the counter, in every possible nook and cranny. 'Did you used to watch Tiswas when you was a nipper?' That was the cue for the burgers, sausages, pies, mushy peas to splatter the pavement.

We heard the car pull up by the side of the van, knew who it was without thinking. Two doors slammed in unison and Mr Skankster, escorted by an enormous gorilla of a man, graced the scene. Since I'd last seen him Skankster had gone upmarket. He stood surveying the holocaust dressed to kill in an immaculately tailored suit, hair slicked back in the style of an old school society gent. He grimaced with disgust at the carnage while the henchman, a locally notorious bouncer, fumed and boiled at his shoulder. 'It's a work of modern art. It'll be worth millions. We've been discussing works of modern art.' The feigned innocence deserved the proverbial Oscar - or a bang on the jaw as the itchy fisted Kong would likely see it.

'Jamie, I'm bitterly disappointed with you.' Skankster's mock regality would have been pathetically hilarious if not for the menace of his lackey. 'Exactly what do you think you are doing drinking in my time?'

'Your time?' The camel's back snapped. 'Your time? I'm always in your time. I'm sick of being your fucking slave, you...you...greasy haired shit!'

The eyes of the henchman narrowed. Jamie reciprocated with a glower of wayward hostility. Clint Eastwood and Lee Van Cleef squaring up for the grand finale, an all guns blazing showdown. 'Young man, Mr Jacobs, here, will be most upset if you refuse to

64

show due respect to your employer. I would suggest that you are not capable of dealing with a man of his size. Think about it.' Monkeyman grunted and shuffled, spoiling for a bone-crunching bout. The warning appeared to cultivate a satisfactory level of intimidation; a juvenile mask of sulkiness was fixed on Jamie's face. Skankster snorted with smug derision. 'I'd much prefer to discuss matters such as these in a civilised manner and in more comfortable surroundings...' My stomach churned, the old crook was milking the elder statesman malarkey to a degree that would make a Colombian cocaine baron, elected to the presidency on an anti-dope ticket, puke. '...But as that seems nigh on impossible at this present juncture, I shall explain. As you may or may not have heard, I have recently become involved, financially, with a number of local clubs and nightspots...'

'Where'd you get the dough, paedophilic porn?'

The insult registered, was acknowledged by a condescending stare from one, a threatening snarl from the other. '...As I've considered you to be one of my most reliable servants over the past few years, I was preparing the pleasant surprise of relieving you of your present duties and offering the prestigious position of bar manager. For that reason I'd asked you to work tomorrow evening.' Skankster paused for dramatic effect, the deluge from the skies dripping from his oily barnet like filthy pondwater off the ugly duckling's plumage. 'Imagine my dismay at finding you drunk on duty, just as I'd telephoned to break the good news.'

Sullenly, Jamie mulled over this twist in events. One of two things was clear. Skankster was either a liar of indecent virtuosity or the feeding of five thousand on a few fish butties had been eclipsed. 'You'll tell me anything, you dirty fucking liar!' Jamie had not believed the boss.

'Jamie Moore, you leave me with no alternative other than to withdraw my generous offer of promotion and have you and your garden gnome ejected from my premises. Mr Jacobs, I think this is more in your line.' But before the minder could place one foot in front of the other Jamie had snatched the breadknife and began brandishing it, leering a promise of anarchy. 'Come near me, any of you, and I'll fucking kill you.' Jacobs stopped dead in his tracks, glancing quizzically at his governor. His governor, a man who maintained a foolishly misplaced air of dignity. 'There really is no need to go this far. You will only bring trouble onto yourself. What the hell has got into you, anyway?'

'His wife's left him. He's been in a state all night.' My eyes were superglued to the raised weapon. My heart began pounding a primal beat.

'My wife's left because that bastard has me working day in day out for sweet FA.'

'Jamie put the knife down.'

'Be a good boy, put the knife down.'

'Fuck you.'

A small crowd of bystanders had spilled out from one of the nearby pubs onto the drenched street. Amid the excited chattering throng a man held a mobile phone to his ear. Jamie saw him, reached the self-evident conclusion. 'The frigging police won't save you!' With astonishing poise - like a man stone sober not hazily drunk - Jamie sprang onto the counter, through the service hatch and dropped surefooted onto the junk food mash paving stones. Skankster's cool evaporated like a chunk of ice thrown onto a bonfire. He slipped in the garbage heap of food while shamelessly scrambling away to safety. Someone jeered. Someone laughed. Then things got crazy. The commotion provoked in Jacobs an imbecilic, ill-timed lunge with his fists. A flash of harsh unforgiving silver swished through the air...the scream of torture was spine-chilling. Clutching his lacerated features the giant sank to his knees, rivers of blood gushing down the backs of his hands. Forming a macabre and microcosmic ocean of vengeance on the pavement before him. Jamie victoriously postured over his defeated quarry. A demented warrior in faded denim. 'This is what you get,' he spat to the horrified onlookers, 'if you fuck with me!'

To the sound of wailing police sirens reverberating through the night air and witnesses screaming terrified abhorrence...Jamie kicked and stamped on the devastation of agony that had seconds earlier been a ominous colossus. It was a murderous onslaught. No-one rushed to Goliath's aid. They saw the vicious gleam of bloodstained steel clenched in bone-white knuckles and understood every grim nuance of fear.

I entered a surreal netherworld, a dimension that had never known gravity. I neither perceived my hand rest on the counter and heave-to my weight, nor my feet collide with the floor. A stark photograph of Jamie's twisted face made repugnant by cruelty and derangement - like that of a possessed beast in an epic horror movie - is permanently scorched onto the retina of my mind's eye. There is an inexplicable cacophonous explosion that ricochets earthquakes through the stability of consciousness. My feet kick out and flail with sheer blind terror; I am a newborn abandoned in deep, murky waters. I experience a white hot sensation in my chest. My legs become insensible and cannot support a disintegrating body. Against concrete my face cracks. There is clarity in sound; brakes screech, footsteps thud and clump with the purposeful, uniform perversity of jackboots. And all the while a soul enveloping nausea. I am devoured alive by eternal blackness. Absolute disorientation. Faster than the speed of light or sound I am an atom travelling through the vast expanse of a godless, meaningless universe. Momentarily I am bedazzled by the profound inferno of a supernova. The blackness returns and becomes a dense, syrupy swamp. I struggle to swim with every last iota of strength I can muster, it is not enough, and I become submerged. Just as my lungs feel they will gasp their last a vacuum opens and I fall headlong into it. Instinctively I know I will never hit the bottom. I plummet through the void for what seems to be a lifetime. It is the horror of the worst imaginable nightmare. An apocalyptic torment. For months afterwards I will wake in the dead of night, dripping with sweat because of this foreboding abyss. Then...I hear it. The soft, soothing voice. More tranquil, magical and uplifting than a choir of a thousand angels. The soft, soothing voice coo-cooing a mantra. A dove of everlasting enlightened peace. 'Everything is going to be all right. Everything will work out fine.' A gentle hand caresses my forehead and I inhale the lifeforce of cold, sharp oxygen. I am restored to the land of the living. I taste an equal dose of blood and vomit. Pain is excruciatingly overwhelming.

'He saved the other man's life.'

'Are you willing to make a statement, sir?' A multitude of noises and faces whizz and whurr, in and out of focus.

'Where's the fucking ambulance?' Familiarity. The voice was mine.

Supermarket

Supermarket, a bastion of democracy. Multiple choice questionnaires guaranteeing choice of multiple conformity. Putting the free in freedom, though the grimaces at the check-outs tell a different story. Put it on the Visa, darling. First six months interest free - eat now, pay later.

Gospel voices above yoghurts and angel delight. From hidden speakers American soul classics float, ostensibly giving the place some. Soul, that is. However, plugging on the small screen vintage R 'n' B has already proved a commercially viable additive. BING-BONG over the sax solo. 'Can Mrs R Matthews please contact the manager's office?' An Orwellian orator on E's.

On and on it goes. Efficient and economical. Dehumanising and basic human needs. Copy the Yankee, copy the Japanese, stir, simmer, set. Hybrid Anglicised cake and eat it. Or have it rammed down one's throat.

Expressions of numbness and glumness: the distant detached politeness. Etiquette shattered only by market-day and weekend rush-hour stock trolley races. Crash 'n' grab the goods. The battle of wits not to be last in the queue at the till...It all begins when a bumbling neurotic bumps into the trolley of everyday Mrs Perkins, unsettling the finicky, delicate order within. Beneath a benign exterior of neighbourly normality smoulders trolley rage, a medically unrecognised cousin of the more notorious 21st century anger that possesses road users. Aaaarrggghhh! The fury rises. Mrs Perkins, identifiable to many as a retired librarian, seethes and fizzles like the vengeful villain in a whodunnit novel. Thus the OAP belligerently completes her circuit of the store. Glaring at immovable obstacles, cussing under fake smiles and deliberately clipping the food-transporters of other customers. Mayhem and madness. Ha! ha! A taste of their own medicine. And the resultant domino effect. Bump, bang, bash, barge and insincere apologies. Life in the fast lane. A throwback feeling. Hunters no more but gathering. Sweeping the shelves with a diluted bestial instinct our forebearers focused when spearing wild boars.

Pork chops six for the price of four.

The aftermath, mechanical Sundays, Mondays and Tuesdays. A hollow backdrop of bland synthetic top 40 hits and an uninterrupted intake of conveyor belt automatons. Robotically plundering the endless, undiminishing displays.

Science fact and horror show fiction. David Jones, a regular Monday shopper and community cared for schizoid, envisages blood dripping from other consumers' mouths, particularly, predictably, by the meat counter. 'Zombie flesh eaters,' David describes to the psychiatrist, Dr Baskite, on visits to hospital as an outpatient. From these hallucinations the dedicated doctor tries to read penetrating insights. Whatever; he continually fails to articulate a coherent diagnosis. Dr Baskite sighs, reads the records for the thousandth time. Pen chewed pensively, another sigh. Inveterately insane or vegetarian visionary? Mental or misunderstood David Jones has recently taken to wearing a large crucifix whenever he steps out to purchase his groceries.

Robots and zombies. By Thursday there is life, of a kind. By some strange quirk of fate Mrs Docherty of leafy Beech Crescent is forever reacquainting herself with the past. She stands, obstructing possible means of escape with her consumer chariot, and imparts her life-story to every last drivelling detail. This week Mavis Grace, a woman Mrs Docherty has not had the pleasure of nattering to for twenty years, is the recipient of the self-indulgent news. 'David was promoted to chief engineer,' so begins the broadcast. Mrs Docherty speaks with an adenoidal whine; perhaps it is the sound of her voice that so distresses company rather than the better-than-the-Joneses banter. 'Lovely floral curtains in the dining room.' Her tongue is inexorable and painful, the sound only an operation or Stanley blade could cure. 'Ever so proud of my two sons, postgraduates, the pair. How are yours?' Breathing space at last.

'Fine.' A junkie convict and a factory worker. Mrs Docherty's arthritic knee trembles and twitches. With an unfaltering, faultless sixth sense she knows when the offspring of her peers have not scaled the same heady heights as her own siblings.

'Blasted woman!' Snaps Mavis Grace in the bus station an hour later. Mavis has missed her bus, the next a whole tedious, boring, dull, tiresome forty-five minutes away.

Recognising a face of thunder when she sees one, the teenage truant takes a step back from the timetable, a precautionary measure in the event that the middle-aged one might take out her grievances on an innocent bystander. The schoolgirl, Victoria Saddleby, is relieved and pleased when her own bus arrives just five minutes later. Slouched on the back seat, puffing on an illicit fag, she daydreams of meeting up with her boyfriend. Love makes the world go round. Mavis Grace, for want of anything better to do, inspects the contents of her purse. Lack of money can make the world seem like it's stopping.

The bus pulls away, leaving Mavis to reminisce that she didn't like Mrs Docherty the very first time the pair met, years ago, as office clerks in a now defunct pop factory.

In the present, here, today, the store detective watches the shop lifter. The shop lifter watches the store detective. Tom and Jerry without the nine lives and mess.

Fridays. Clunk-click. Acceleration. Gearing up for the weekend. The weekend workers put the foot on a psychological pedal, burning away their jealousy of those lucky enough to be blessed with days off. For those with days off this day drags torturously on. Home time expectancy becomes unbearable. Suzy Roper and Gav Marshall of the bakery and butchery departments are bursting with ambivalence, fluctuating between thoughts of headbanging walls and party pill popping. For months their eyes have met in mutual admiration, tonight they have arranged a clandestine date clubbing in Leeds. Only

Madge Cook of the check-outs knows. Until, that is, Madge secretly confided with, one by one, over half of the store's employees. 'Between you and me,' of course.

Urban Deprivation
From The Palace of Wisdom

Here we are at the place of knowing in the middle of a world of shit, as usual. It's Wednesday and the rain is smashing the road like 50lb mortars. Jimmy slowly exhales a huge cloud of smoke from his nostrils then bangs the bong down on the table splashing stinking water onto the toast I'd just made. A typical Palace of Wisdom moment.

The Palace of Wisdom was a phrase coined some other time. The Palace was a basement flat in a four story house, not too luxurious, but not a shit tip by a long shot. There was a box-like gas fire situated on the wall with mahogany look top and sides, a huge Hendrix poster hung above it flanked by smaller ones of pro-skaters. A heavy wooden table stood in the corner with a small, green, pot table lamp in the corner of that. A soft two-seater sofa sat in the middle of the room covered by an Afghan throw-over twinned by another in front of the window, purchased in Afghanistan funnily enough, by Jimmy, the kid who lived in the Palace. Behind the sofa in the middle there was a small kitchen with all the modern gadgets crammed in. The stereo stood lonely in the far corner of the room with a bong next to it that Jimmy had made from a large Jack Daniel's bottle.

We called it the Palace of Wisdom after a lengthy conversation we had one night. We were talking about how fantastically touching *After Christmas Blues* was. A Mersey Poem. Another mate, Hip Hop, was talking about the *Odyssey* and how much it had blown his mind, reciting whole paragraphs in a Richard Burton style voice. Then there was one of my other friends describing the end of the Hendrix song

Axis Bold as Love, and the feelings that it evoked in him. I thought this was a totally mind blowing three way conversation and just had to point this out.

'Just imagine trying to have this conversation with any of the meat heads up town.' There was a loud roar of laughter.

'You'd get your face kicked in and then some,' laughed Hip Hop, 'if you're not talking about football or shagging, the meats are not interested, it's a fact of life.'

And this was true. Very true in our town.

You couldn't talk to your average Joe in the pub about anything of substance for fear of getting beaten up. You're a puff where we live if you're into real music or art. That's how the meats see it, so you do your best to avoid them at all costs. Real music? Hendrix, James Taylor, Mother Earth, music that comes from the soul, even folk, the Incredible String Band, John Martin, Dylan, stuff that isn't sugar-coated and produced.

'Watch what you're doing twat I'm eating that.' I like my bongs and I like my toast, but some things just don't go together.

'Shut your shite man,' he said, eating my toast as well. Cheeky bastard. I was too stoned to come back with a stinging retort. My mind wandered in and out of distant memories for a while and started to walk through the door marked 'Amazing sex with Lisa' only to be rudely interrupted by a loud knock at the door. It was my good friend Hip Hop. He was a tall lanky fucker with a chip on his shoulder about coppers and a penchant for art. He likes to read, and he has a habit of reciting stuff back at unusual moments just to freak you out.

'Alright people' he said, flashing his perfectly chiselled whiter than white teeth.

'What you looking so fucking pleased about,' exclaimed Jimmy, gesturing with his arms in the air.

'Well brother of few positive words, I have just acquired a cheque from the tax office for the modest sum of five hundred English pounds, and am about to embark on a drinking session of mammoth proportions. Anyone interested in coming with me on this fine day?'

'I don't know about fine day, it's pissing it down,' piped up Jimmy.

It certainly looked like it might suddenly become a nice day with an offer like that and who am I to turn it down. We were in.

The rain stopped hammering the tarmac and the clouds opened to let the sun through.

'That's our cue,' said Hip Hop, pointing through the window towards the sky.

We all got up to hit the pubs of town. 'Into the great unknown, to oblivion, to the ends of the earth.' I could hear Hip Hop shouting loudly as he disappeared out of the door in front.

It smelled marvellous outside. I always loved that smell, you know that smell just after it had rained. I don't know why, it just smelled clean and fresh. Listen to me, I sound like a fucking washing powder advert but that's me, always going off on tangents. Hip Hop was marching up front spouting some poetical shite, (well I say shite but I was probably one of the only people that appreciated his ramblings) and I brought up the rear with Jimmy as he locked up the Palace. So there we are snaking through the dilapidated streets like lambs to the slaughter, on our way to get slaughtered, with THAT FEELING in my gut. That feeling, a kind of nervous tension right in the pit of my stomach. Don't get me wrong, I loved going drinking in town with friends but I could never forget where we lived, how we acted, who we were. Yes these were dangerous times for people of our kind, people who were even slightly cultured. To get through a session in town without a fight or confrontation was always a bonus. So as you can understand it was incredibly difficult to shake THAT FEELING.

On to the traffic lights where a car screeches to a halt at the other side. I recognised it. It was Dink, the tight one.

'Where you lot off to, into town?'

A muffled 'Yeah' was mumbled back at him.

'I'll meet you up at The Light then' and sped off.

'He's probably on the tap,' said Jimmy, looking slightly pissed off.

He really got to Jimmy more than the rest of us, even though he did our heads in as well. Dink isn't a meathead by any means, but the thing was he'd always spend as little money as possible to get by. Even though he had a job and usually more money than the rest of us put together, he'd never splash out, never treat anyone where as the rest of us were more like a family. If one of us was hungry or thirsty, one of the other lads would sort them out even if it was their last bit of cash. But not Dink, he was the kind of cunt that would let you starve even though he had enough cash in his pocket to sort you out big time. Trust him to see us when we were busy on our way to spend Hip Hop's five hundred finest English pounds.

Let me get this Dink thing off my chest. One night everybody was going out into Leeds. I had no cash and was really pissed off because I couldn't go, but Dink was hassling me. I kept saying 'Stop fucking bugging me I'm not coming I'm skint' but he was determined. 'Come on, come on I'll lend you some cash.' He kept on at me for what seemed like an eternity until I cracked.

'ALRIGHT ALRIGHT! Give me the money ya moaning bastard I'm fucking coming.'

'Right, I'll get you some from the cash machine in Leeds,' he said.

This made me feel a bit uneasy but I went anyway. So we tip up in Leeds, Dink has done a body swerve to the cash point straight away. 'Nice' I thought, he's usually a twat you see. There's me and this guy B Boy standing on the corner with a couple of birds and Dink reappears, and hands me some money. 'Are we off then?' and starts walking off down the street with the birds. Me and B Boy slowly follow, I unwrap the notes to see how much he's given me. He's given me a tenner. The anger starts swelling inside me, I'm out for a night in Leeds and he's given me a tenner, a fucking tenner. I'm thinking, what kind of a wanker is this bloke to think I can do a night out in Leeds on a tenner? I restrain myself so as not to make a twat of myself in front of the birds. Anyway, we do a couple of bars and the tenner's just about gone but I'm starving and so is everybody else. Dink suggests we go to a burger joint. Agreed!

Cut to the burger joint and I say to Dink, 'Buy us a burger then Dink.'

'Get a fucking job,' he sniggers and then laughs at the girls.

This really pisses me off. I bite my lip and laugh.

'Come on man I'm fucking starving.'

'Piss off,' he sneers, colder than a dead fish in a cryo freezing tank and laughs at the chicks again.

This was his thing you see, he loved making you feel shit in front of folk, making you look beleaguered and small just because he had a few quid. Especially in front of women. I did my best not to blow up and kick his fucking balls up his back. I shrugged and walked out in disgust. I couldn't believe how anyone could be such an arsehole so I kept about ten paces in front of him and the two mixed-up femmes on the way up to another bar.

'MOJO' the sign flashed above the door, I remember thinking I hope mine's working 'cos I'm gonna need it tonight. They were way behind me by now, I had enough for another beer, so I thought fuck it and just went straight in. I got the attention of the good looking barmaid and ordered myself a bourbon. She was smiling at me as if to say come and have a go if ya think you're slick enough. And I would have, but my concentration was broken by Dink and the chicks' loud laughter as they entered the bar. I turned to look but as I rotated my head I caught sight of another mate, Mick. He saw me and shouted me over.

'Alright C,' he smiled gesturing to the barmaid to get me another drink, I fucked Dink off straight away and made my way over to Mick. I started to run over the evening's events, Mick couldn't believe it, screwing up his face only interrupting occasionally with comments like 'tight bastard' and 'what a wanker'. Mick gave me some money to get some food and so I did.

Anyway, even though Dink isn't a meat by any means, that's why he's not a regular in the Palace and he has to cruise the streets looking for us if he wants to come out and play.

We arrived at the pub. It was at the end of a busy high street in town which was always jammed with double parked cars. 'THE LIGHT' it said on the sign outside, I always thought this was pretty ironic because you could hardly see a thing inside, it was so fucking dimly lit. It was a pretty run of the mill pub inside, you know the kind with that thick red and black Axminster carpet with the horribly dated designs on it and those long oak look bars with a long brass pole fixed all the way along it at the bottom just to rest your foot on in case your leg started to ache whilst in the middle of that long and arduous task known as buying a drink. There were two pool tables in the back and a kind of covered over Mediterranean style terrace outside with those trendy new outdoor heaters that were kind of like lamp posts with gas burners in the top under a sort of steel brolly. Pretty crap really but that's just where most young single sexually starved lads (and birds at that) went to drink.

'What sort of beverage do my friends require?' asked Hip Hop at the bar. Jimmy decided for all of us as he sometimes did, 'Pint of Stella and a Jack Daniels and Coke.' The barman did his deed, we all bollocked down our bourbon and proceeded to take our seats round the pool table with our pints.

'Rack 'em up then' chirped B Boy.

I was still pretty stoned from the bong hits earlier so I didn't realise that he was talking to me.

'OY fuck nut' I snapped back realising he was looking at me, 'do ya wanna game or not?'

I started setting up the balls as Dink sailed through the doors to meet us.

'Alright lads, how's it goin'?' He used to put on this crap Manc accent like Johnny from that film *Naked*.

'Not bad, Dink not bad.'

Dink took a quick shifty at our full pints and could probably smell the Jack on our breaths.

'Where's mine you cunts?'

This was fucking typical.

'You getting a round in then Dink?' asked Hip Hop.

'I'm not, no.'

'Fair enough then.' Hip Hop steamed back to the bar without argument. He brought us all a double back but left out Dink.

'Where's mine?' moaned Dink, 'And where have you got all the money from?'

'I got five hundred quid tax back but you, you can fuck right off.'

I could see him looking puzzled, he couldn't even work out how he had pissed off Hip Hop. I sat there looking at a dejected Dink, thinking of that time in the burger joint and all the other times he had pissed me off, glowing with laughter inside. Take that you bastard I thought, what goes around comes around. It didn't happen much but when Dink got a taste of his own medicine I fucking loved it.

So the hours started to fall away and we were all getting pretty trolleyed, and there's a few more folk starting to gather in the pool area. Hip Hop is talking to these chicks and (as usual) charming the tits off them. He starts reciting poetry to them in a very grand old English voice. The girls are loving it and laughing loudly when this thick-necked dude at the other side of the pool table, with a white shirt on and a bit of a tash, throws an empty cigarette box, which bounces off Hip Hop's head. Thick neck and his mates all start barking with laughter, Hip Hop turns about face and in his most well spoken accent says, 'Ha bloody ha, very intelligent for a Neanderthal.'

They all stare back looking puzzled for a second, then one of the other blokes, a guy with love and hate tattooed on the backs of his fingers and Sheila tattooed on his neck pipes up, 'Fuckin' poetry. Are you a pufter or summat?'

'Why, are you looking for a date?' replied Hip Hop. That was a pretty dangerous thing to say, and straight away you could feel a tension in the air.

'Are you callin' me a puff now?'

'I wouldn't dream of it, a red blooded homosapien like yourself, no.' Hip Hop said in a super sarcastic tone. Then thick neck started again, 'He's calling you an Homo Baz, a woofter, a queen, a faggot, an arse bandit, a shirt lifter, he's saying thy's fucking queer, I wunt stand for that.' I could feel things getting out of hand, someone was about to get hurt and I'd a feeling it wouldn't be Baz and his mates. I made a bee-line for the bar as I knew the landlord, Fat John. I quickly explained to him what was happening and it looked like he was gonna help me out. When he clapped eyes on the blokes I was talking about, an expression appears on his face that says to me he's just shat himself, then he started stuttering and mumbling, 'I...I...can't help you son, you're on your own' and scurried off back behind the bar.

'Thanks a lot John, you twat.'

Against my better judgement, I went back over to try and resolve the situation without too much bloodshed. I get back over to the pool table and the geezer with tash and tats has got Hip Hop by the throat and is just about to knock the shit out of him. I have to admit I was fucking bricking it but I couldn't let my soul brother get leathered. I approached them and put my hand on the meathead's shoulder, he spins round and grabs me.

'Wo wo,' I say, 'he didn't mean owt by it. A big lad like you would do him no problem we all know that.'

My mind was racing as I tried to humour the meathead 'Save yourself, have a pint.' He dropped us both.

'Strongbow, and the same for them' he says pointing at his three mates.

'No problem man, no problem.' I shot to the bar and got the cider for the meats, scowling at Fat John in the process, then shot back over and gave them the drinks. I signal to the lads to get the fuck out and so they do. As we walk away I hear one of the meats saying 'See ya bummer boy' in a high very camp voice. Hip Hop turns to say something back looking really pissed off, but I grab him and drag him out of the door. I figure humiliation is easier to take than a fractured skull. The others don't see it that way, but they all came round eventually, apart from Hip Hop who was fucking livid and quite understandably so. He was ranting uncontrollably about nazis and fascists so I chilled him out with half a joint of skunk that I had in my pocket which I was saving for later. I started to console him, 'Cool it man, look at it this way those pricks in there have already given us our regular dose of ignorance, violence, stupidity or what ever you want to call it, so just chill and enjoy the rest of the evening. Hopefully we can have a steady night now without any more bullshit.' The THC coupled with my little speech seemed to do the trick. So we zig-zagged on our merry way to the next shit hole.

I was in a three way conversation with Jimmy and Hip Hop about how we could improve our predicament and life in general, mine was the fame angle you know with the band and that, Hip Hop was spouting off furiously about how the world would be a better place without uncultured numb nut meathead fucks as he called them and Jimmy was rambling on at a hundred miles a second about how music and art could have a definite effect on society given a push in the right direction. I loved this, this was my thing, talking about real issues or what I considered to be real. We used to talk about things like this for hours in Jimmy's flat, the place of knowing, or as Hip Hop very nicely put it one night 'The Palace of Wisdom'. This was a great metaphor for the place we all used to smoke at, it might sound a bit elitist and maybe it could be construed in such a way, but to me we were wiser than the average Joe on the street, maybe not in an academic sense but in a spiritual sense if you get what I'm saying. I mean take your average meathead for an instance. You couldn't talk to him about art, real music or literature, he'd probably kick your teeth in before you got to the end of your sentence in our town, so this is the on-going battle that my team had to face daily. I've a feeling I might have already mentioned this, but you know now how it gets to me.

So everybody is getting well pissed by now, it's getting late so we move to one of the town's night spots, the name is not important but it was the usual type of place found in ex-mining towns in the north of England with the usual three or four testosterone-ridden gorillas on the door. One of the gorillas had a huge square head on top of his massive shoulders and greeted me in an almost inaudible tone 'Dun't cum in them fuckin' trainers next time orayt dick 'ed.' I nodded and slid past him avoiding eye contact, you had to take their shit you see, they were the bouncers and you were the punter, and if you didn't like what they were saying you could fuck off or they would kick ten bells of shit out of you before you could say large donner with extra chilli please love, you just had to take it. It was just easier that way.

Inside the club is packed, the dj is playing some horrible Euro pop remix of a song that wasn't that great in the first place, there's a few other people there that hang in our social circles including Jay, the magic man. He sees us walk in and comes straight over.

'How's things C, you alright?'

'Yeah not too bad Jay, these doormen are still shits though.'

'Oh forget about them twats come and have a drink.'

So we all took seats in the foyer, it was a kind of narrow walk way with tables and stools on each side, with a gap down the middle leading to some double doors which in turn lead to the dance floor. Jay was entertaining (as usual) telling us this hilarious story about how his dog was once in the local paper because this old dear from the end of his street had mistook it for a wolf and attacked it with a cucumber. Whether it was the truth or a lie it was still a good story. He always kept us entertained Jay, that's why we called him the magic man, he could breathe life into any party, no matter how dire it was. He always had this massive smile on his face, he was a real good guy, not aggressive but he had this I don't give a fuck attitude that always seemed to work for him. Anyway, the evening was sliding away nicely until out of the corner of my eye I see the block headed gorilla saying something to B Boy's girlfriend. I found out later that he was asking her to move her stool out of the walk way but she didn't hear him, understandable really what with everybody talking and the crappy music blaring out of the speakers. Then I see him bend over and put his mouth right behind her ear and shout at the top of his nastiest voice, 'MOVE YER FUCKIN' CHAIR YA SILLY COW.' She turned round startled and probably scared. 'What, what?' but before she could finish the gorilla had picked her out of her chair, slammed her into the wall and with his huge hand slapped her across the face. B Boy immediately sprang to his feet to stop the bouncer's assault on his woman.

'What the fuck ya playing at man she's only a...' but before he had finished speaking he was slammed to the floor by two other gorillas and thrown out of the door head first taking a few kicks and punches on the way out. Before I knew it everybody that was out with us was involved in the ruckus. A massive argument ensued outside in the precinct and I'm thinking this could get really nasty seeing as it had gone outside, those bouncers could be evil motherfuckers, and if provoked in the slightest way they could really fuck you over and get away with it. So against my better judgement I decide to go out and try to calm things down, then Dink appears from the toilet unaware of the madness that had gone on, approaches me and asks where everyone has gone. I tell him what's happened and he walks towards the door to check it out. BANG! One of the bouncers tackles him, knocks him to the ground then punches him in the back of the head, and I mean these are not small men and no matter how much Dink pissed us off he didn't deserve this. It was well out of order, a trickle of blood rolled down the back of his neck from behind his ear as the bouncers ushered him out, they threw him into the street like a discarded piece of rubbish. A startled Dink picked himself up and dusted off his clothes. I could see the initial shock wear off and turn to rage in his face, he picked up the first thing to hand which was a big wooden sandwich board advertising taxis, waving it around above his head like a madman. The bouncers cowered back into the doorway like frightened children.

'You bunch of brainless bastards' he shouted, launching the sandwich board at the door with all his might. It clattered the doors and the bouncers scattered then came piling out of the door with one thing on their mind, BLOOD, Dink's blood. Then all at once it hits him, he's just challenged four of the hardest, most violent men in an already violent town to a fight. So what does he do, well what do you think he does, he turns and runs like fuck. There's a black mariah at the top of the precinct, so with the bouncers chasing him he heads straight for it. We all had a pretty dim view of the coppers including Dink, but if there was ever a time that he needed their help it was now.

'Mate, mate they're gonna kill me, they're gonna kill me.'

One of the coppers, a big one with a dodgey too-big tash stopped him running.

'Steady on son, what's up.' His voice sounded kind and I thought maybe he would diffuse the situation like a happy old plod should, but then the bouncers caught up. Blockhead was the spokesman but now he had another two blokes with him, two that were not at the original incident, a small stocky black guy and a big skinny bloke that I'm not even sure worked on the door there. Blockhead said to the copper, 'This lad has just thrown a bottle at me endangering the people in the doorway.' Then the coloured guy chirps up, 'He called me a black bastard and a nigger as well.' This was total bollocks, I was there, none of that shit happened, he threw the sandwich board yeah but the gorillas didn't even mention that. The big copper's eyes started to narrow, he looked at Dink twisting the end of his huge tash, Dink springs to his own defence. 'That's bullshit man they hit me for no rea...' SMACK the copper hit Dink in the gut with his truncheon, Dink collapses on to one knee, he doesn't know what's going on but as he looks up he sees Blockhead winking at tashy as he walks away. The Rozzers bundle Dink into the back of the van and lock him up for the night.

Hip Hop is totally outraged and starts ranting at the police. 'I demand to know the reason for detaining this man, I've never seen such ludicrous behaviour.' The tashy copper leaned out the window 'Shut your fucking mouth dickhead or we will have you as well.' 'Have me, have me, I think not, I am Agamemnon, Lord of the War Cry, warrior to the gods.' The copper looked back at him in disbelief, to say he looked confused would be the understatement of the year. He was totally puzzled to the point where he didn't even reply and just drove away.

This incident just instilled more hatred and distrust in the police force for all of us. How come he goes to them for help fearing a kicking from the bouncers, gets one from the police then gets locked up. I for one fail to see the justice in that.

The conversation on the way back to the flat was, as expected, about what had just gone on and pretty garbled due to the drink and what ever else had been consumed. We were pretty near the flat now, by the time we got in Jimmy had already got three skins together and was bitching about the coppers and the bouncers. I had lost all of what little faith I had left in the establishment and was running over the events in my head. 'Does anyone know how that happened?' I said questioning everyone.

'All I know is one minute we were sitting having a beer, the next my girlfriend has been assaulted and I've been beaten up for trying to stop it, what the fuck is that all about?'

Then Jay pipes up 'What about that shit with Dink, I know he's a bit tight but that was well out of order, no one deserves a hiding for walking out of the bog.' Even Jimmy was defending Dink, 'If those cunts had done that to me, I would have thrown more than a fucking sandwich board, what is it with those guys?'

The initial shock from being man handled by the thugs was starting to wear off B Boy's woman. 'What did I do to provoke the bouncers, why did they hit me? I just can't understand it.'

'You did nothing to provoke them, they are just morons on a power trip, they just have some kind of morbid obsession with inflicting pain on people. The scary thing is, they get away with it.'

'I'm inclined to agree' I said 'even the coppers are at it, did you see the bouncer winking and laughing as he walked away, and they expect you to take their shit quietly because you're pissed so you're automatically in the wrong, it stinks man, small town politics get right on my tits.'

'Yeah just look at that poor fucker the bouncers nearly killed in the supermarket car park,' said Jmmy, 'they kicked the shit out of him then put a Pils bottle in his mouth and jumped on his head.'

'There's no need for that' said B Boy, 'my point is that everybody knows who did it, probably the coppers as well, and the twats got away with it without even a fine or a slap on the wrist.'

'I mean you don't even have to be involved in anything to get the shit kicked out of you these days, if you draw the proverbial short straw you're fucked, even if you've done nothing, it's like playing Russian roulette,' added Hip Hop. We were seriously mulling over, coming down from yet another assault.

'Come on people, take it easy, we are now safely back in the Palace of Wisdom, fasten your seat belts and prepare for lift off.'

Jimmy was building one of the fattest joints I'd ever seen and upon passing it round the room a couple of times the team eased down.

'That's better, is it not?' exclaimed Jimmy between smoke rings and slipped on *Sweet Baby James*. 'Lonely by day empty and cold only to say lo and behold.' What a fantastic record I thought and started to discuss it with B Boy. 'Too fucking right, what a beautiful melody and how the fuck does he generate so much power in the chorus on acoustic guitars with no drums, it's absolutely amazing.' Everyone has got a spliff now so I dim the lights and get comfortable, JT is weaving his beautifully crafted melody through the air and we all talk, play guitar, sing, tell jokes and so forth. Hip Hop is back to his old self and is talking about the book *Stepenwolf* by Herman Hesse, comparing the magic theatre to an LSD trip he'd once had when suddenly the conversation was broken by an almighty crash.

Someone had thrown a can of paint at the window. I went cold thinking that maybe it was the bouncers coming back, to finish the job they had started in town only this time without the assistance of the coppers. Fuelled by alcohol B Boy kicks off. 'Who the fuck dare's to throw paint at my window?' and he's striding towards the door but we all grab him, 'Don't go out there man, you could get killed.' But there's no stopping him so he just walks out…but there's no one there, except out of the corner of his eye he sees next door's door shutting.

'You bastard' we all hear B Boy shouting.

'What is it?' I say.

'It's the fucking cave man from next door.'

The man in question was Dangerous Dave, B Boy was constantly battling with him, he was a real fuck nut, he always wanted to fight someone when he was pissed and he was pissed more than he was sober, but you could usually patronise him into going away without him knowing that you were taking the piss because he was a bit slow. Nevertheless he was a big bloke, hence the name. So B Boy goes and starts banging on his door telling him that this time he's gone too far etc.

Dave appears at the door. "Wadayoufukinwant.' Dave is pissed out of his head, (nothing unusual but you just know there's gonna be trouble when he's that wrecked.

'I'll tell you what I fucking want, I want you to get your stupid, thick, Neanderthal ass down there and clean that paint off my window.'

We're all stood watching, there's a short silence then B Boy chirps up again 'Well are you gonna clean it up or what ya wanker.'

That did it, Dangerous Dave is out of the traps like a greyhound, he cracks B Boy a beauty in the face and knocks him into the street, B Boy gets back up in time to stop the second barrage of punches from the dangerous one, then hits him back in the chops. Jimmy's had enough so he tries to split them up but gets punched in the process. This pisses him off no end so he starts lacing into Dave. Then Jay gets involved and tries to break it up. By this time Dave's wife is out on the street and she's going ballistic, then the kids are out screaming, 'No, no Dad give up' and she's wailing at the top of her voice 'If he gets sent down again you're all fuckin' dead, do you hear me, I'll have you fuckin' knee-capped.'

Now all the lights in the street are coming on one by one, this is too much for me on a Wednesday night, it's absolute chaos and I'm just about to fuck it all off and go home when Carl walks round the corner. He's a big, nasty, hard bastard but he's my mate, which is nice, and not only that, he doesn't like Dave very much. So I run over to him and ask him to sort out the cave man. He agrees in an instant as he's just had an argument with his girlfriend and needed to offload some aggression. So he walks over, casual like, pulls the rabble apart and knocks out Dave with one sledge hammer like punch. And that's it, it's all over just like that. The screaming kids and wife chill out and start to pick up Dave from the street, blood gushing from his nose and mouth. The wife looks up, 'I hope you're proud of yourselves.'

'He threw the paint and he threw the first punch, he's only got his self to blame. I only asked him to clean up his shit' and with that B Boy went back into the house so we all followed him and smoked until we passed out.

I woke the next day with a headache the size of the Empire State Building and a half smoked joint on my chest. The fact that I could have burned myself alive didn't enter my head, I just thought 'bonus' and proceeded to light it up. The rest of the team were all strewn across the room like corpses and were waking up in unison. 'I feel absolutely shit' was the general consensus as they coughed themselves back into the world of the living. It was Jay the magic man that uttered the eternal words that were ever present in the Palace of Wisdom, 'Who fancies going for a pint?'

'Fuck it, we might as well all go I've still got plenty of cash left' yawned Jimmy. Here we go again, I thought.

Face Arranger

I let him finish his piss; made out that I was straightening my collar. Then, when he was zipping up and lovey-dovey posing in the mirror, I did him. Grabbed his long student hair by the scruff and rammed that know-it-all mug crash into its own reflection. Wowzer! He didn't see it coming until it was too late. He had a real shock-horror expression when he did click on. All in the blink of an eye, as they say. Fucking hilarious without a shadow. Yes, too busy fancying himself pretty boy was. Silly cunt would have trouble pulling birds from now on.

Fucking blood was everywhere. At first I thought I'd slashed one of my hands on a piece of broken glass the stuff glugged out that fast. Better than anything I've ever seen on any eighteen certificate. Real life drama. Ruined my new shirt it did - so I booted him in the bollocks.

I would have stood, all casual like, and admired the lovely chaos I'd created. Probably chucked the odd wisecrack into the bargain if it wasn't for Deano. Deano was always a bit of a worrier. 'Fucking hell Mezzie you shouldn't have done that! You said you were only going to slap him around a bit!' Fucking panicking Deano boy was. I could tell by the way his eyes were like slap-up dinner plates and by the way the treacherous twat emphasised the word 'you'. 'Shut up soft cunt,' I remarked, Kray cool like.

'We'd better get out of here. That's a stretch, that is.' Deano stared at my butchery couldn't-believe-his-own-peekers style. Could have knocked the cunt over with a feather (could knock the cunt over with a feather at the best of times but that's beside the point). Like I said fucking blood was everywhere. So I've got to admit Deano had a point about the possible legalities. 'Somebody'll come in soon and recognise us, hurry up.' Deano was ready to run. No nerve at all. He hadn't even done anything. Peepshow freak.

'See you later shit-breath,' I spat at student boy - not literal like, but I would have done if I'd have thought on at the time. Student boy didn't reply. He was out cold from my predator-like ambush. That or the soft cunt had fainted. Can't stand the sight of it some folk. Especially when it's their own. I gave bookworm a leaving present - another kick in the balls. Too generous for my own good.

His blood stunk worse than the piss in the flooded pot, I'll tell you that for free.

Slipping out of the joint unnoticed was easy-peasy. Saturday night, darkened pub, disco lights then strobe, bodies doing the sardine samba - you know the score. The bouncers were busy; conveniently hassling some loser they didn't like the look of. So getting past them was no bother. Not that bouncers bother me. It's just that there was two of them and I've always had my doubts about Deano's ability and reliability as a back up. Wouldn't want to be in a trench alongside the prat, put it like that.

We jogged across the main street in case the plods were snooping; they weren't. None of the losers wobbling from pub to pub would have noticed my guilt soaked shirt either. They were all too busy ogling, cheering and booing a pair of rat-arsed birds that were flashing their tits at a passing taxi. Get gang-banged tonight them two would. Not by me mind, I insist on a bit of class. Most of the time.

Anyway, we made it to the safety of a dark alley pretty sharpish. Best thing about this town, there's plenty of alleys to disappear down whenever the need arises. And the need often does. No brags, no bull, but I can be a naughty boy every now and then. Heh-heh.

'Jesus, did you see all the blood? Fucking hell.' I could tell Deano was really, really shitting a brick. If I hadn't needed the prick's help I would have dropped one on him. Disgraceful display of cowardice it was. But I had urgent needs and Deano's flat was placed perfect to cater for them - nicely central you see. Gets ripped off with the rent if

I remember rightly, but that's his problem. 'We'll have to give your pad a visit. I'll have a quick swill, you can lend me one of your shirts and then we'll be as right as rain. Back out, few more beers, then meet the boys down Keeks.' Couldn't stand the thought of the night ending early - fucking bongo bashing the beat-up in the bog had been. The speed was a real racy buzz too. Purchase some more of this excellent substance I promised myself.

Deano, the non-stop whiner, tried pissing over my fireworks. 'Fuck me Mezz, that was way over the top. All he did was laugh when you dropped your pint.'

'Teach the pillock not to be such a smarmy bastard in future then, eh?' No way was I going to let Deano poop my piss-up. I let him know as well. 'I FEEL LIKE A PARTY!' I shouted into the darkness. My words echoed between the alley walls, a total special brew sound. I did feel like a party as well. One where I could really let my hair down and rip-roar wild. After a week-load of work-shite giving way to the more animal instincts is just what the doctor ordered. Or should that be just what the vet ordered? Anyway, you ought to try it sometime.

Bit of a philosopher me, as you're no doubt beginning to appreciate.

Deano lit a cig. Anxious Deano was. He was puffing on his fag like a bloke who had two zonks left in the world and couldn't decide whether to back a horse or buy a pint with them. I could tell by the way the ash-end flashed on and off like Flamborough lighthouse. Went to Flamborough on holiday when I was a nipper. Fucking boring; worst holiday I ever had.

'The law pulls you in, no way was I involved.' Wimp.

'Give us a cig you tight cunt.' He did. He even lit it for me.

'Do you hear me? I didn't know you were going to do that. I'm not involved.' I'd left student bastard in an ugly mess. Worse than I'd realised. I could tell.

'Fucking-fucking-fucking hell. You really shouldn't have done that.'

'Watch your fucking language you hysterical cunt.' He didn't laugh: miserable fuckwit. 'The coppers won't catch up with us. Stop fretting. The pigs don't give a flying one. Everyone knows that. Just another Saturday night incident to them.'

For a while Deano put tape over it. We walked single file down the alley; me, king of the jungle; him, fly on the turd. What with the whizz it was a tricky business keeping my tit-licker still. I had plenty to wax lyrical about - like my lethal victory over the education system for one thing. But I knew if I talked Deano would too, and I couldn't stomach that right now. Spoil the magic of the moment his voice would.

I had to laugh when Deano slipped on a crushed beer can and went flying. Slack git. Can't hold his ale. Doesn't even have to tip the frigging stuff for it to put him on his arse.

I could tell my laughter hurt his feelings. 'I don't think we should go back to my flat. That'd make me some sort of accomplice.' He brushed himself down after picking himself up.

I couldn't believe my fucking ears. Of all the lads I had to be out with Deano. Nothing short of a disaster that the rest of the lads were short on tokens this week and would only be in the night-club. I'd be some sort of hero if the rest of the lads had seen me do the student's face. Not with Deano boy, oh no. Bit of a funny cunt. Never know where you are with him. Deano had always had a bit of a reputation for being a Nancy boy.

'Wait until I tell the rest of the boys that Deano would've sooner turned me over to the law than help me out.' I tut-tutted at the faggot's shame. I really felt like lacing the wanker. Don't know how I restrained myself. Patience of a saint I've got.

My pearl of wisdom provided enough food for thought though. 'All right. Come on. Let's be quick about this. I don't want my collar felt for this. It'd put my job in jeopardy.'

It rarely gets better with Deano. Bash my bishop, him and his poxy bank job. Fucking cashier the be-all-and-end-all. Wouldn't mind if he was an advisor or some sort of important fucker but all he does is count out grannies' copper jars. 'The only good bank jobs involve shotguns.' Not that I'd know. Just up for a bit of fisticuffs, yours truly.

Back in the flat Deano didn't let up on his moaning and groaning. Trying to get me to stick my head in the oven or something daft. 'Mezzie you're always the same. Don't think before you act. Not that

98

I'm adverse to a ruck, but you always go too far.' I fucking liked that. Don't think? He's the slug-slow - the stories I could spread. Adverse to a ruck? He can try talking posh as much as he wants but some of the boys take Deano to Leeds games and give me more than match stats. 'Yellow-belly boy' the footie lads always call old tough guy Deano.

I never go to the footie. Fucking poofter sport. Idiots sitting and staring round Satellite screens as if their lives depend on it. Dim twats paying fucking fortunes to watch some arse-wipe mummy's boy millionaire kick a bag of wind about. Then start a fight 'cos the silly cunts they follow can't hit a barn door from two yards. Fighting costs me next to sweet F.A. Couple of pints then deck some sucker, that's my motto. My dosh is for more important things, clothes and what not. Fucking well turned out all the time I am. Top designer gear no less. Birds go for a trim and tidy bloke. But football, like I say, fucking poofter sport.

The powder was the best stuff I'd had for ages.

'You go fighting at football don't you?' I splatted a zit in the bathroom mirror - can't allow splashes of margarita to ruin my playboy pin-up, can I? Deano pondered while taking a slash. Didn't look so I can't confirm whether the rumour's true. Supposed to be hung like a porn star Deano is. Doesn't know how to use the fucking thing if he is. It wasn't a bird who started the rumour, two of the lads de-kegged him when he'd had one over the limit. The rest of us are a tad sceptical about what they claim to have seen.

'Well...er.' Anyway, I had the cunt stumped. He didn't want to admit he chickened out on the soccer hooligan stakes. Ruin the image nobody believed in.

'Some heads get cracked after games don't they? That's what you lot always tell me.'

'Well...'

'Always said football was a poofter sport.' It's true. Every time I hear some pissed up tosser mouthing off about battles with Millwall I have to do the prat, unless it's one of my close associates of course - they're exempt unless they fuck me around. Can't stand toe-to-toe these footie fans, they never last long. Perhaps I never meet the real deal hooligan so to speak, but I've still to meet a footie fan who can hold his own. Football, I fucking hate it.

(Though between you and yours truly if you tell the birds you watch the occasional England match it does no harm to your chances. For some reason birds like watching England. Fuck knows why, we always get whipped by the fucking foreigners even though we invented the game. Like cricket, but that's a fucking poofter sport as well. This country's going well down the pan...told you I was a thinker, didn't I? Ought to put me in politics. I'd give all them hi-class hookers a lesson or two in love.)

Deano was still freaking - the wet fanny. 'I'm sure one of his eyes was hanging out of the socket.' I couldn't take much more of this:

'Will you shut the fuck up?' He did.

I swilled the blood off my arms and hands. I must've held onto student geek's head for a bit after I'd boffed him. Couldn't remember properly. Did him proper though. That I could remember. Deano's deodorant and aftershave made me smell like a queer. Fucking tasteless he is.

I noticed the slimy shit didn't loan me one of his best shirts. He wouldn't have got it back if he had. Only fair, soft lad needed punishing for tonight's piss-poor performance. The shirt fit all right. We're about the same size in body if not in spirit, though I've got muscles, well toned. Look good on a beach I would. I work out. Deano is a bit of a lard-ass.

Deano is also a bit of a woman. 'Nice place you've got here, darling' I said scragging my hair just so in front of this posh ornamental mirror thing in the hall - I'd pull tonight, no doubt about it. Couldn't help thinking what a selfish sod Deano can be; he doesn't invite the boys round here that often. I grinned, I'd soon put a change to that. Would have to see if I couldn't arrange some sort of raving randy knees up. 'Like a fucking hotel this place is. Fucking definitely got the feminine touch you have, Deano boy. I'd marry you if you had better legs.' All mod cons, more stuff than Comet - washer, video, microwave, stereo, dishwasher, new carpets, new curtains, you name it - the full works. Even looked like the loser dusts and hoovers up regularly. I think Deano is what my dear old ma would call a nice boy.

'If we pull a pair of lucky ladies bags shagging in your bed, you can have the sofa. My back's played up all week at work.' Got to bullshit every now and then, it does no harm. Deano said nothing. 'Right. Sorted. Spiffing. Come on, let's get another drink.'

'We're not coming back here,' Deano mumbled. 'I'll burn the place down before that.'

'Long as you pay for the matches, skinflint.'

We left his mangy flat.

I couldn't wait to meet up with the rest of the lads. Deano was that long-faced anyone would have thought it was him who'd been launched through a mirror. The cunt's that ugly he's probably used to breaking mirrors without head-butting them, mind.

Not once, but twice, he blew our chances of getting off with a couple of slags. They weren't grade A floozy but we could have had them back at his flat for a bit of slap and tickle nevertheless.

'What's up with you?' I asked when the second pair of ugly bitches gave us the elbow. It was scandalous, it really was. Deano hadn't uttered a single word, leaving yours truly with the chore of all the flattery lark. If I'd have been successful I'd have had his keys and had a threesome. He could have gone fuck his fingers in the park. It wouldn't have been so bad but the cunt usually bored you senseless with sport talk. He'd probably have scared the women away if he had have opened his gob, but it's not making the effort what gets on my tits. Never one for the ladies, Deano. Don't bend down when the cunt's around, is what I say.

For some reason he was all edgy and nervous. He was getting on my wick. Luckily I had a brain wave and decided to drag him to a quieter pub. He needed talking to, sorting out. No intent to do anything underhand, just a fatherly in his shell-like. Not the wisest of blokes isn't Deano. A tin of beans short of a skidmark.

I placed two red bull and vodkas on the table. 'Pour that down your prattler. Liven you up a bit. Could've been in with those birds you know.' The wanker had a real cry-baby look about him. Never again with you matey. It'd been the same walking over to this dive. There'd been this pissed up cunt, tottering all over the pavement he was. Nobody else was about. Just me, Deano and this pissed up cunt.

101

'Probably the father of six kids,' I told Deano. 'Fucking wrong it is, going out, pissing it up the wall when there's kids to clothe and feed.'

'How do you know he's got kids?' I'll tell you now, I didn't like that tone of voice:

'He's got a fucking fatherly look, that's how I know.' Fucking scrounging off the welfare state no doubt. You can spot the twats from a mile off. 'I'm going to lamp the loser.' I would have as well only:

'Oh for God's sake. Just let's get a drink shall we? Let his wife sort him out. It's fucking boring this. Can't we just enjoy ourselves?'

'I am fucking enjoying myself. Or would be if you had enough spunk in your balls. And you shouldn't take the Lord's name in vain I'll have you know.' My Auntie Pat's a Catholic. Bit of a plastic Catholic - she shags all over the place so she must be on the pill. There isn't sprogs all over the place is what I'm trying to say. She doesn't have the rest of us paying for family allowance.

'Well I'm having a shit time.' They're all the same these limp wrists who can't lay it on with the split-arses. Blame anything or any fucker except themselves.

And now, liberty of fucking liberties, he was ignoring me. 'I said, we could have been in with those birds you know!'

'Don't feel like it tonight.'

'Do you ever feel like it? Sometimes I wonder if you're a shirt-lifter.' He said nothing, just sipped on his drink. Yeah, the one I bought him. Tapper. 'Night-club next?' Once in I'd jettison this drip right away. The rest of the lads wouldn't be there for an hour or so but maybe one of the sluts would come up trumps; have an ace between her legs, like. One of the best things about this town, there's plenty of sluts. Like getting my end away I do.

'You think you're so fucking hard you do.' The beer was going to Deano's head. It often made him go all bitter on you.

'Relax. Just a bit of action that's all. A few stitches and he'll pass as being fit. Plenty would have stuck the boot in more than twice before legging it you know. Went easy on him, I did.'

'He was having a piss. He had no chance. It was fucking cowardly, that's what it was.'

Fucking liar. Student twat had put his cock back in his jeans. 'You'd better watch your lip, you had.'

Deano went all sulky again so I jigged over to the jukebox. Didn't like the way things were turning out; this was Saturday night for christsakes so I had to do something to lighten up. The bastard jukebox took my money and didn't give me any credits. So I stuck the boot into it. What else could I do? 'Watch it! Watch it! That thing cost good money.' This was the landlord speaking. He was waving his arms about like he intended to take off. 'Don't lay an egg mucker.' The jukebox was one of those 70s style things. Landlord tight twat had probably bought it from a second-hand shop. 'And for your information it's just taken good money off me without giving me any credit.'

'Justice.' He thought he was a funny man. Normally I'd have directed my drink and glass at the wanker but I couldn't trust Deano to do a Linford. He'd have probably sat there waiting for the law and confessed all. It didn't put me in the best of moods though. It wouldn't, would it?

I stared at the landlord, then the middle-aged loser propping up the bar. There were only two other customers, a couple of grandads who weren't worth bothering with. The landlord, a fat git with a beard, stared back. The loser at the bar looked the other way. Smart move. I'd have done him if he tried anything bright. One wrong move and his lights were out.

'Drink up and out.' This was landlord fatso, obviously. I ignored him, to Deano I said:

'Night-club then?'

'What for? To watch you smash some other poor bugger's face in.' He sat there looking at me all stroppy. What else could I do? I slapped his cheek with the palm of my hand, not that hard, but his cheek stung red. 'Cheer up,' I ordered. Got to let the weaklings know who's boss every now and then. Keep them in line.

'Out!' The bar-belly had taken a definite dislike to me.

'We're going.'

Fucking wide-boy thought he could out stare me. When we got to the door I threw my glass at him full pelt. The glass missed by miles but knocked the clock off the wall at least. Bad shot or no bad shot it was worth it to see the landlord and the shagless mug at the bar duck. I didn't give a fuck. Never went in this poxy pub usually anyway. Fucking ought to be condemned, it did.

We were ten yards up the road when the landlord came storming out swinging a baseball bat. Wouldn't have thought the big bopper could move so quick on his feet. 'Right you cunt,' he growled and slobbered like he needed quarantine, 'let's see you being clever now.'

Got to admit it, it fucking scared me a bit. Gave me a dose of the heebie-jeebies: him with the baseball bat, me armed only with my wanky fucking fists.

'He did it! You saw him! It's nothing to do with me! You saw him hit me. He's a fucking bully, that's what he is.' Deano had just put his head in a noose.

'Right,' the chip chomper said to Deano, 'you fuck off. I'll sort this nasty piece of work out with a lesson he'll never forget.'

Deano the deserter legged it.

Big bother here brother I thought. Being a man of no small intelligence it was as plain as day that I couldn't rely on any knight in shining armour - a mate in adidas with a jagged glass. Apart from the beer being crap and mein host being a toilet the dump was so dead because it's the sheet on the end of the roll, so to speak. Fucking spoils a good pub crawl coming to this shithole. No good for a big night-out reveller. A backwater of sewer water.

I used my conk and started backing off real steady eddy: mad fuck landlord followed my footsteps, as if he was an old-time dance partner. Half-a-chance I'd really tread on his fucking tootsies.

I could tell he really meant to do me, truly I could. His face was screwball snarling and he held onto the bat like he was holding his dick just before the vinegar stroke. Intense, that's the word.

'Leave it out Dennis, leave it out. You'll only land yourself in it. Have your license removed.'

It was one of Dennis' endangered species; the regular-at-the-bar who had followed and was now observing proceedings from the comfort zone of the pub doorway.

'Nobody comes in my pub and throws a glass at me. Nobody.'

His goat was really up. Dennis the bastard looked a menace all right. But where there's a will there's a way, somehow I knew I'd find a way to gnash him.

I kept using my conk, staying schtum; concentrating. The speed was a lifesaver. Two steps back to every one step forward of the menace.

'Dennis you'll land yourself in deep water. Read about this sort of thing in the papers all the time. Bloody louts getting off scot-free while decent law abiding citizens get the book thrown at them just for defending their own property.' Cheeky cunt, who's he calling a lout? It's the wogs, spics, dagoes and pakis that are ruining this country. Every fool knows that.

Anyway, the loser-in-the-doorway's words had some sort of soothing effect on dear old Dennis. Not fucking common sense mind. Maybe they're bum-boys who do Yoga together or something poncey. The fat menace stopped, tossed the situation over in his mind for a few secs, then pointed the bat like Zorro facing one of his arch rivals. Zorro looked a bit more agile understand. 'Come near my pub again and I swear I'll fucking kill you.' Dennis beady-eyed me to get his point across then about turned. I hate these cunts who think they're John Wayne in the US Cavalry. OK Dennis had a similar figure, but he would have been just a bit too much. Would likely have broken the trusty steed's back on mounting. Pity his wife, know what I mean?

Life, it's a funny old thing. Some people just don't have a clue. Take Dennis, he was a first-class fool and a lead-head loser. Two for the price of one. Come on, nobody threatens me with a baseball bat.

Even if I say so myself, I was quick. Dennis still had his back to me when the first punch landed, high on the side of his head. It was a beauty too. A real sneaky sidewinder. Dennis, the silly old cunt, staggered sideways and my knee was breaking his nose before you could say 'flabby fat fuck'. The baseball bat clinked to the floor at the exact same time as Dennis' dung-dropper touched down. I grabbed what little left he had of his hair and one-two-three jab jolted his bonce back. No more than five seconds all this took. Bruce Lee couldn't have wiped a Sumo out quicker.

When I let go Dennis' dumb nut cracked hard against the paving stones. Need an anadin or two in the morning old bean, I thought. 'Ever threaten me with a baseball bat again and I swear I'll fucking kill you.' I'm not too sure Dennis' answering machine recorded, he looked a bit out of it down there, all bloody and bruised. So I let him be, after treating him to my trademark finishing touch of course. A toe-end in the tackle.

The trouble with these middle-aged twats. They don't realise they can't go like when they were twenty.

The loser-in-the-doorway hadn't moved. You could easily have dumped a dustbin into his gaping gob though. Fucking chicken. I screeched that he was a wanker and the saddo quickly disappeared inside. Straight to the blower, I thought.

After kicking the baseball bat towards a drain - fuck knows why, it just seemed apt, like - I set off at a sprightly sprint. The night was still young, plenty of time for more adventures. I couldn't help smiling. Always look on the bright side and all that.

Should Deano be in the night-club he'd get his fucking share as well.

Supermarket

Jennifer Addison. The kind of check-out girl people who have overdosed on reality believe only to exist in glossy improbable commercials. Young, friendly, polite, caring - breathtakingly beautiful to boot. She is one of life's underachievers. Bright enough to have excelled at school if other girls hadn't bullied her, envious of the precocious but already potent attractiveness to the opposite sex. Currently Jennifer sails with ease through classes at night school. She is desperate to leave the supermarket. It will be the supermarket's loss. Jennifer is a prize asset.

Over afternoon tea pensioners comment to their friends that they were served by such a lovely girl in the supermarket. The charismatic girl restores their faith in youth. Puts a bionic bounce in their zimmer frames. Just a smile is enough.

So approachable is Jennifer that other women - unless they are of the green monster clan - ask the beauty what kind of mascara or hair conditioner she uses. As if they had been friends for years. None realising the check-out girl would stun and shine if she were on a desert island a million miles from civilisation and cosmetics.

Unattached men avoid shorter queues just to have Jennifer handle their weeklies. The young men find it impossible to take their eyes off the girl. They find it impossible to believe that her bewitching beauty is smiling at them from behind a cash register rather than from the front cover of a glam mag. Jennifer, her faithfulness to her childhood sweetheart as powerful as any aphrodisiac smile, spell, amulet the hopeful admirers could ever hope to offer. She used to be flattered by the attention. In an innocent kind of way. But of late she has become wary of the affections and advances of men. Derek Saddleby has taken to calling Jennifer into his office to sexually proposition the bombshell belle.

It is a pity Jennifer's boyfriend went to the other school in town. Maybe she would have been spared.

Limbo   Land

The first rays of the new day's sun creep over the horizon to bombard both retinas in my head with such ferocity I feel my skull will split in two. Then the headache kicks in like a stampeding herd across my frontal lobes. Something's not right.

'You look like you could use a coffee.'

Through a blurry eye I see there's someone standing by the window, she's a vision of perfection in a white shirt. She's fixated on my persona with a provocative - no damn right pornographic - look on her face. She looks Swedish, so much so she is the stereotype. I'm thinking I'm in one of those soft focus, all too perfect, very, very wet dreams that sometimes affect us in that limbo land between asleep and awake. I'd never pulled a woman of that calibre in the whole of my sorry existence.

The sun is warming my skin and lighting up the dust like fireflies. I sink back into my dream pillow and hear words.

'So do you want one?'

The pillow is warm and soft and I feel the pull of sleep dragging me like a lead weight to the bottom of a lake.

'Are you ignoring me?'

I rub my eyes and scratch my head. I'm naked except for a sock hanging from my left toe. I'm grasping for memories of the previous night, the air in the room is thick and there's a woman there I don't recognise. What the hell was I up to last night? I couldn't remember jack shit, not a name, nothing, and I was beginning to freak. The weight was pulling me deeper in to the lake of the unconscious. The situations I get myself in to. I didn't want to offend this woman. She put a cup of coffee by the bed. I started to feel embarrassed by my lack of clothing and pulled the duvet across to conceal my modesty. Her voice floats, I fall away.

I dream of an island with me on a hammock sipping Vodka with fruit juice and a bottomless sack of herb. My only company on the island is a nymphomaniac supermodel who's sole purpose in life is skinning up fat ones for the dude in the hammock. She says nothing but reads my mind, anticipating everything moments before I ask her for whatever. I hear her voice but her lips don't move, she just smiles and echoes in my head. I try to ask her how she does it but before I open my mouth she's already answered telepathically. *What does it matter Jay,* and it all starts to get a bit mad, *as long as we can still fry.* I look across at her quizzically, and to my dismay discover that her lower right arm has turned into a huge black cast iron frying pan with a red and yellow fish in it sizzling in a little oil. Wait a minute I think to myself, I'm the fucking boss of this dream. Then it all started to go really pear-shaped. The island was no more and the supermodel was hideous, chasing me down a long dark corridor, trying to squash me flat with her huge frying pan arm chanting *Jay's dead, Jay's dead.* Fuuuuuck! shouts I, but I'm not making any headway and she's getting closer and I'm out of breath and SLAP!

'Come on man get your lazy ass up.'

There's a bloke in the room slapping my face.

'Come on, up, now.'

He draws back the curtains and the sun explodes into the room making the dust swirl on currents of air. It sounds like my old mate Jack but I can't make his face out. I can't even hear what he's saying. His voice is distant and his sentences melt together like some massive multi-syllabic word. I drift.

I'm in a car on a clear day with Jack. I mean, I say with Jack, he looks nothing like Jack but I know it's him. *This is gonna be wicked man.* He's buzzing and I'm just trying to figure out why. *Soundtracking a Porno, I'm eternally grateful to you for learning how to play that fucking thing.* He points to a guitar on the back seat. *How the hell did you manage to get us on to the set?* This is more like it, I'm thinking.

Well you know me Jack.

And I think fuck it. It's my dream, why not? *I'm always happy to oblige if you know what I mean.*

We pull up outside a reasonably sized detached and enter through the heavy oak door. I come to another door, walk straight in to find a kitchen full of lighting gear and a couple of blokes with small cameras. Jack's wearing a pair of overalls and I'm in the same get up. I have to laugh when I catch my reflection in a mirror and discover that I'm sporting one of the biggest, thickest, blackest, most 70s looking moustaches I have ever seen. A tall blonde and a Latin looking type approach us with nothing more on than a tiny silk slip apiece, they stand there in silence as if to say *Yeah?* (I've seen the fuckin' trailer to this) 'Jay and Jack, we've come to fix yer washer luv.' *ACTION* shouts one of the guys with the handy cam. The sleazy groove of porn funk slides in from somewhere out there. A chocolaty bass, smooth sax and a funky wah.

I sure hope you boys brought your tools says Blondie.

I'm sure we've got a ratchet to fit your socket spurts Jack grabbing his package. Within seconds he's performing sexual gymnastics on top of the washing machine with the blonde. They're going at it hammer and tongs in all manner of impossible positions as it kicks in to the spin cycle. I'm taking control of Latino and am on the verge of an explosion when the dream starts to dissolve and become distanced. No! Not now, just give me another five minutes, one minute even. But it's too late. I'm aware of someone moving about in the room. They've been doing a fry up, I can smell it. Maybe it's my brother. He's shouting something. I can't quite decipher what.

He raises his voice another couple of decibels which is really beginning to piss me off. All I want to do is get back to my red-hot Latin lover and he's probably disturbing me because of something really dull, if indeed it is him at all.

The back door slams and I immediately slide back in to the comfort of unconsciousness.

I'm swimming with the fish in the depths of a blue ocean. Shafts of sunlight are diffused by the water and dance all around like ghostly spectres. Huge beds of Kelp sway and dance in the current filled with

115

a multitude of shell fish and eels. I breathe the liquid and it feels cool in my lungs. I float along without a care in the world trying to work out the significance of all the fish and why they keep appearing in my dreams. A Barracuda swims up to me and says (in fish speak of course) *How the devil are you Jay, and how's life on the other side?*

I'd rather live down here to tell you the truth mate. It's beautiful, serene even. Everything is so complicated, laborious and well just plain shitty up there.

For some reason, this really pissed off the Barracuda. He trebled in size and started to take on the characteristics of a bad mother fucker drill instructor and started to scream. *You are never happy with anything, you are a total slacker.* His presence became all the more menacing and was starting to scare the shit out of me. *Slackers like you need to be broken. You need discipline. You think you're under pressure in that pathetic life of yours, I'll show you pressure.* And with his massive jaws grabbed one of my arms and headed straight down at terrific speed. First my ears pop then the air is being squeezed from my lungs. Panic sets in, I can't breath, my rib cage is starting to crack, my face is purple, the veins bulge throughout my body and AAAAAGGGGGGHHHH! I wake covered in cold sweat. There's an untouched cup of Coffee on the table by the bed. My girlfriend Jenny is stood at the sink washing dishes. She looks great with the light coming in through the window and I'm so glad I'm not dead. I feel as though I've had a week of insanity, I'm so tired and I haven't even got up yet. She turns to face me.

'You all right Jay, you've been tossing and turning for hours.'

'I am now babe, I am now.'

'Your Dave's been round, trying to get you to go fishing with him but you were dead to the world so he just went on his own'

'Right.'

I sleepily sound back. I start to feel content once more and slowly but surely slide back into the blackness of sleep.

Survival Instinct

It all happened so quickly. I didn't know what to tell *anyone*. Most things wash by me, days go by without me noticing a thing. I'm in a trance and I drift. But there are moments that are triggers to change. There are moments in a situation when you are so awake, so conscious and clear headed and your brain works so fast you can see the whole of life in an instant, you can look back on the path you have drifted and see every turn and every mistake. It's in those moments when instincts come into play, you pledge an oath to yourself, never, absolutely never, again.

I woke up at twelvish and came round about one, maybe half-past. It had been a late night. There's an office across the street, and the dozy bastard who worked there had left the door open when he went home. I had fuck all else to do so I let myself in and started playing on the computers and using the phones. Not on my own like, with a mate, Roger, a rich kid that had lost it in his head, fucked up somewhere early on in life, couldn't cope. We were buzzing, heads rushing, we'd had a bag. I don't say that coolly as though I always take that shit, I don't, it's just a matter of fact, I did it, and I'm certainly not proud. I've seen how far that shit can go. But when you're short of kicks, of a buzz, then you take what you can get. Anyway, we were playing away, next thing you know, it's late. Then all of a sudden it's twelvish and there's a rehearsal.

I was in a band and we rehearsed in fits and starts, but at that time, we were doing quite a lot. We practiced in my bedroom when I lived with Roger, so I thought I'd go and get the front man, he wouldn't have got there otherwise. Anyway, and I don't know why I did this except that my head was still in pieces from the night before, and the hazy ones before that, but I can still see the moment so clearly, above all others in many ways. I got in the car, and that was it, things were gonna happen.

It was an easy task considering. It had only been broken into a couple of weeks back so the driver could get in just by putting one finger into the void where the lock used to be. It wasn't my car, it belonged to Roger, who was still fast asleep. There was no need for keys either, which was handy, you just had to lift off the plastic on the steering column, dig in to the spaghetti of wires hanging out, put two together and it was off. Hot-wired and all that. What the fuck was I thinking of?

I should point out here that I can't drive – I was going to say 'to save my life' but that wouldn't have been funny. When I say I can't drive, what I really mean is that I can drive, I've paid plenty of attention when I've been a passenger and figured most of it out, and I ride my bike on the road, it's just that I haven't had any lessons or passed my test or anything.

I felt alright about it. I reversed the car out and I could have shot straight off, but I was careful, and it was only because I was going steady that I saw him coming down the street when I spun to face the journey ahead. I noticed that someone, as well as me, had remembered to come and practice. It was Norman. Our drummer. Bumbling along.

'What you doin'?' he asked, all jolly and fresh.

I told him that I was going to pick up our man. Without doubt or hesitation, Norm got in the car. What the fuck was he thinking? He knew I couldn't drive, I was certain of that because we'd talked about it more than once. I used to tell him how much I wanted to be able to drive and to have my own car, and feel all good and achieving. He'd moan at me about being banned. They took his licence off him for twelve months for getting arseholed and swaying down the road only to be met with flashing lights in a lay-by. Stupid bastard. He had gotten off lightly too. And with all that, he still didn't seem bothered about me driving, not at first anyway, not when he just got in. When we were stationary. Everything was alright then.

We set off. I was cool, or I thought I was. I was going through the gears and being confident, but not cocky, I knew I had to concentrate. We got down the end of the street and out on to the main road. It didn't take long for Norm to get nervous. It must have been how I was driving, I thought I was cool, but when I felt his nerves, they sort of made their way into me. I felt his tension double when he saw me light-up a cigarette and start driving one handed. If you're gonna drive you might as well be cool about it, make the most of it. I was through the gears, second, third, I got a bit of a rush when I got into third, then when I hit fourth everything seemed a hell of a lot faster than it normally did.

His nerves were burning into me, I swear it, and that's what set me off and set the whole thing off really. He made me feel less sure of myself and that's what led me to swerve past a parked up Fiesta. I'd glided past loads of parked cars and would have done with that, but he was putting me off, and I was a bit spooked and all of a sudden I wasn't sure I'd left enough room to get past. I swerved and panic filled the car, on-coming trucks, cars, bikes, pedestrians were suddenly hard to keep track of. If I had to pinpoint a moment, I would say that was when the real trouble started. The first doubt.

'Slow down man, fuckinell you've got to do it really steady.'

He was gabbling.

'Just glide out until you've past it then glide back in again.'

'Norm, calm down a bit man, you're shitting me up.'

He did. He was silent. Real noisy silence. The void created by him not speaking left open a massive crack for all the normal, scary sounds to rattle in my head. I could hear the engine, obviously. I could hear the rubber tyres rubbing against the road. I could hear all the bearings rolling against each other, I could hear how badly lubricated they were. I could hear the tension in the suspension springs. Birds, passing cars, I could hear so much. Every individual sound crisp and precise. Each one clear and distinct from the other. Each one burnt into my memory. I must have been tripping or truly shitting myself. Fear washed into my head, it was like a liquid, a tidal wave. Everything I could see was vivid, bright and technicolour. The grass verge was so green, and I could smell it, like it had just been cut. Proper doubts were well in place.

We were just rolling away and there was a moment through the silence where we thought we would make it. I'm saying we, because I'm talking for Norm, I knew what he was thinking, I swear it. There was telepathy, I could feel his head in mine. But we were cool for a while, everything would be fine, the worst was over. It was a thirty-zone and I was doing forty, we acknowledged that that was a shrewd move, if I'd have stuck to thirty, then we would have been obvious. I got a buzz from it, looking back, I can remember actually enjoying that time, that lull, when we were safe, in the face of it all, we'd pulled through and I was cool and I was hoping people would see me, hoping to be noticed. We rolled into my hometown, where I was born and raised, a lot of people knew me and I felt right. I had temporary fantasy fulfillment, like in those moments when I talked to Norm about driving and wanting my own car, this is what I thought it would be like. Pain and pleasure, they are so close, they are inseparable.

We came down a hill and round a bend at the bottom and looked out into a little straight with traffic lights at the end. I felt Norm tighten up again, 'It's the fucking lights man, it's the fucking lights'. I don't know if he was thinking it or I was or that we both were, but I was nervous again. Calm was over and the forces that be, which just before the bend were in perfect harmony – me, the car, the road, the momentum all tuned together – were now in discord. It wasn't just the lights, but I had to turn right and the road split into two lanes and I had to get in the right hand side. Now I knew what to do, but I also knew that this was one of those situations where it would have been useful if I could actually drive for real. If I was on my bike, I would have ducked out, banked on to the pavement and missed out the whole mess. But that wasn't an option.

'Do you know what to do man?' buzzed Norm, trying to hide the shake in his voice, which just made it weaker.

'It's alright man, don't worry.'

And it was. I drifted right, there was one car in front of me in my lane, and cars started to pass me on the inside, they were going straight on or turning left into the estate. That was weird, cars going past on either side, this was a real driving situation, but I was fine and if the truth be told, buzzing off it. It was intense.

'Slow down man.'

I didn't need that. It was just enough to break the spell of my concentration and doubt flooded back in. The car in front of me was getting closer fast. Fuck, I did need to slow down, the lights were red and the car was a few hundred yards in front of me and I could have stopped easy, but then the lights went and changed and I could see the guy set off and I felt the tension drop. I couldn't believe it, a green light, and I would be round and that would be it, it was no problem from there. Safe again.

A cunt coming the other way jumped the lights, cutting up the guy in front of me and made him reach for his brakes. I saw the red lights come on at the back of his car, two great big red glows was all I could see, it was like I was staring straight into the devil's eyes.

'SLOW DOWN, SLOW THE FUCK DOWN, FUCK, FUCKING HELL.'

Norm lost it. I went straight for the brake with both feet. I could have stopped I know it, if I'd used my head and gone down the gears and braked heavy I would have stopped I'm certain. But Norm was screaming like it was all over and the Devil's eyes were getting closer and my feet were hard on the pedal and I thought fuck.

And then I did what disturbs me the most. I gave up. That was it, I delivered myself into the hands of fate. I took my feet off the brake, clenched my fists and made my arms into an X in front of my face. Protect the face, that's all I felt I could do. I'd been on the edge the whole trip and the moment came where I no longer felt capable of intervening. I gave up. Totally. And this is what scares me, in that moment, with my arms in front of my face, hurtling towards collision, what was at stake, what I had given up on, was my life. I felt the moment of death. These were my thoughts, I saw myself as a child, I saw my family, I saw the bag and I saw darkness. In the very last moment I saw my ultimate error and I have not stopped seeing it since.

There was a jolt and an awful bang and a metallic crunch that started like someone had stamped on a milk carton. A big fucking milk carton. I don't remember much about that sound, it's all a blur. Thankfully, something took over, and I just didn't listen to it, or if I did, something wiped it straight out of my memory. Whatever instinct did that for me, I am eternally grateful. All I can remember is a moment of calm, I was alive, I was unhurt and so was Norm. Relief just swept through every single fibre. Whatever had happened, I was alive, and nothing else mattered. Whatever was instead of death. And that is some fucking buzz, not to be dead.

My view was pure blue, the bonnet was laid on the windscreen, it looked like a big clear sky right in front of me. I opened the door and stepped out onto solid road. I confronted the situation, fuck knows how I did this, by walking up to the car I'd crashed into and checked on the people inside. As I came alongside the driver's door and peered in to see the dark crimson blood run down his face, my heart sunk and my head flipped. I saw the blue sky again, only this time I was on a beach with my own store, a thatched little open fronted Caribbean number selling watermelons. I'd figured it all, the way out, every single step, and accepted my new destiny, to be away, to have run. The scar created by that very moment would never heal, the task of talking my way out of it appeared beyond even me, with a lifetime's experience of a seemingly never ending string of situations that required plenty of talking out of. And there I was, on the beach, with my own hut, a pile of watermelons, a big knife, not talking about what took me there. My future reality. His voice brought me back, and filled my head again with that vision of blood and wreckage.

'Shall we get the cars off the road?'

He was calm. Very calm, considering. Shall we get the cars off the road? Wait a minute. Shall we get the cars off the road? I can't drive. I haven't a licence. The car was stolen. Who was driving? They didn't know.

'Norm, you're going to have to move the fucking car man, I can't do it, I'll look a right twat, pull it over Norm.'

Norm bounced the bonnet down, jumped in the driver's side and started fiddling the wires. I jumped in beside him. No need for that, I can see now, but then, I was on a thinker, if he was going to drive off, I was going with him, he wasn't going to leave me there, stood near all that blood. Norm was fiddling like crazy trying to hot-wire the car. They were watching us, the bloody folk we'd crashed into and the nosey bastard by-standers. Two young punks, ramming the back of a car and then hot-wiring their banger back into life. It was obvious we'd nicked it. Norm couldn't get it going. I leaned over, all eyes on me, stretching over Norm, I could just about reach, I put the wires together and it started. He pulled it over and bumped onto the kerb. The front end of the car was mashed, it wasn't going anywhere fast.

So there we were, on the kerb. The other car pulling in behind us. A small crowd had gathered, watching the little thieving bastards in their hot-wired car squirm like fuck. That's when I wished I wasn't me. Now what? I looked at Norm and he looked at me. Pure telepathy. We both dropped our shoulders, yanked the door handle and we were off. Legging it. Very fast down the street. Every ounce of me was given to the pursuit of speed, as fast as I could, every morsel, every breath, every drop of blood giving it for speed. I'd given up once, minutes before, gave up on my life, made a cross with my arms and left the rest to be, but not now. Everything about hummed in harmony, go, go and go.

I heard four things. I heard my feet pounding the pavement, I heard the whistle of the wind as it rushed past my ears, I heard my breath, in and out, and I heard my heart pounding, thu-thump, thu-thump, thu-thump. This was the buzz, the ultimate buzz, it was instinct, the survival instinct, it felt primitive, urging me on from deep within, get out, get out, away, away, nothing else entered my mind, just that one thought and everything combined to the action. This was the buzz all right, the ultimate buzz, better than anything. Survival. That's what we do. That's all that we do.

We cut through the estate, through ginnels and backways, over garden hedgerows and all kinds of obstacles to lose the trail of anyone stupid enough to follow us. All the while tired and hurting but never once thinking about stopping. We ended up in some grotty municipal park in the middle of a housing estate and sat on the swings to get our breath back. We just sat there rocking gently back and forth, heads bowed down and our legs dangling loose and free. We didn't speak. We didn't think either. We just sat there. Numb. Down.

Roger was still asleep in bed when I got back. As far as he knew the car was still outside waiting for him. I wasn't going to tell him otherwise. It didn't take him long to accuse me when he found out. I denied it, but he didn't believe me. Called me 'A fucking lying thieving arsehole shitbag' if the truth be told. After a couple of weeks of unbearable tension, I think he'd even told the cops he thought it was me, I confessed to it all. I wore a tie when it came to the trial, I smiled sweetly at the magistrates, first offence and all that. The judges were lenient, digging old people's gardens and having my dole docked every week was going to sort me out apparently. I paid the fine eventually and I did the service, it wasn't that bad, it washed by me, I was in a trance most of the time. As I said, there are moments when you are so awake, so conscious and clear headed you can see the whole of life in an instant. The big smudge that is the rest of life can also make you forget just as quickly.

Supermarket

The bimbo factor. Saddleby doesn't realise that beauty can have a brain. He doesn't realise that he is this beauty's unwanted beast. 'There could be a supervisory position in the offing young lady.' Jennifer knows that Saddleby is lying. Not that the truth would make any difference. 'Name the date, pick the place and I'll pay for the hotel. What your boyfriend doesn't know can't hurt him.' Saddleby stares into the girl's contracting pupils, self-assured, empowered, unctuous. He ogles her chest. The girl looks away, anywhere, finding comfort in the sight of her sensible work shoes. She flushes with an hatred that is mingled and subdued by dazed mortification. 'I don't think I should. I've been engaged for two years and...'

To the preying pen-pusher the strain in Jennifer's voice betrays shyness and weakness. 'Playing hard to get,' Saddleby sneers, 'but think of all the things a man in my position can offer you that your boyfriend can't. Young Simon Powers, your fiance, works in the box factory. Wages not so high, not much of a future.' Like everything is a corporate transaction.

'How did you...' Her voice trails away again. Glancing up for the briefest of moments she glimpses Saddleby's prurient gaze. Then she stares at her laces once more. She feels frightened. Saddleby has been checking up on her. Like some sort of stalker.

'In my business it's my business to know.' The tone is that of a crash course tutor of sales technique.

Twice in this situation Jennifer has despised her indecision. She desperately wants to tell Saddleby where he can stuff his job, but, at the same time, she is shackled. Beloved boyfriend Simon and she have been saving for a deposit on a house they have both set their hearts on. There are not many better paid jobs on offer at the moment. She has sent plenty of unsuccessful applications for the ones that are.

Maybe Saddleby is right. Everything is a transaction.

Saddleby rises from his chair, gleefully rubbing his hands. He removes his wedding ring and casts it into the waste paper basket, a moronic grin gnarling his features. Like the deal has been signed and sealed and delivery is long overdue. He slithers around the desk, places a finger on Jennifer's chin and lifts her face so that she cannot avoid his eyes. He brushes his lips against hers. 'Think about it,' he whispers.

Jennifer's workmates find her crying in the toilets. She tells them that it is that time of the month. The workmates nod with the empathy of suffering womankind. Jennifer knows she has one hope. The reason she threw a sickie on Monday. Afterwards she had been quite confident. She prays the money has not been wasted.

Saddleby sits at his desk, scratching his nose. He then slips the wedding ring back on his finger, the grand gesture having been made. There ought to have been a character in one of those U.S. soaps based on yours truly, Saddleby thinks. The virility of power. And irresistible it will prove.

Dustbin   Man

I awoke from sun drenched dreams and fantasies to a head full of hangover and the electronic alarm clock screeching in my ear, reverberating through my head. I heard the rain straight away being driven, in fact smashed against the window by a powerful and howling wind. I smacked the alarm clock out of desperation to make it shut up, and commenced trying to separate my mouth from itself. It felt and tasted as if someone had poured a tin of *Evo-Stick* into it. This was a distinct possibility because at the moment I didn't have a clue where I'd been, who I'd been with or what I'd been up to at the weekend. It was five-fifteen am, Monday morning. I was on days. Some sober and moralistic people I know say it's not a bad shift, but I'm a piss head (amongst other things) who can't stand life before eleven-thirty and who finds work mind-numbingly boring.

I lay there in the pre-daylight gloom, trying to get my thoughts together for the coming day, trying to clear my thumping head, but it hurt too much. Normally under these circumstances I would have put my emergency utility action plan into operation, which would have consisted of telephoning work with some shit excuse and ligging it. The last excuse used was that I'd been abducted by aliens (I had been on acid so I only considered this a white lie) but the finalist of all final warnings from the accursed employers had sabotaged the *modus operandi* of this once trusted method of escapism. This meant that I had to rely on my built in auto-pilot automatically automating me in to some semblance of action.

'Brain to body, brain to body, come in body, over.'

I swung my legs off the bed and put my foot in what felt like a plate of chow mein, I couldn't remember buying any or eating in the bedroom, but who knows? Wiping it off on the crumpled Fred Perry on the floor I wobbled to my feet, immediately reeled and wretched whilst the room did three hundred and sixty degree revolutions which put Bonaparte's France to shame. Steadying myself I managed to get dressed whilst looking at the jammy bastardette, the girlfriend who didn't start work until ten, and who shifted and took up residence in the warm spot I had vacated in the arena of lust, the bed.

De-fumigating the mouth came next with the help of Colgate Blue Minty Gel and the electric tooth brush with expired batteries, a quick swill, then breakfast with copious amounts of coffee. I was coming round slightly, but didn't dare disengage the autopilot in case of a crash landing. It also reminded me to take out the dustbin for the bin men, which is where the fun began. I put on my coat and work boots, opened the door and stepped out into the maelstrom of weather. The wind buffeted me and the rain was driving into my face like hailstones. I felt like a Scarborough trawler man in a force ten westerly and I'm sure Ahab would have been happy to employ me.

Grabbing the wheely bin I set off out of the gate and down the ginnel which ran adjacent to the back of the row of houses where I lived. Most of them being boarded-up. I was trundling along pulling the bin and then I was suddenly on my arse on the drenched floor. I thought for a second that my autopilot had disengaged its navigation systems, but it hadn't, it was a saboteur's booby trap. A length of washing line had been tied across the ginnel at shin height. Kids no doubt, or urban terrorists. Apart from being wetter than I previously had been, and extremely pissed off, I was OK. I fumbled around trying to undo the knots that tied it in place, but I couldn't, so I just picked up the bin, left the spilled litter where it had fallen then heaved, dragged, wrestled and fought the dustbin over the obstacle. With the objective gained and bin in place I set off to the bus stop from where I caught a lift with Andy to work. After a twenty minute drive and enduring Andy's conversation about the West Yorkshire Working Men's Darts and Dominoes League, which holds no interest for me whatsoever, we arrived at work. Entering via the gatehouse the familiar gut wrenching feeling of I don't want to be here overcame me again.

Did you know that there isn't a law in England that says it is compulsory to work and yet, through the government and its agency the Employment Services, you are forced to. The law says you need fifty quid a week to live (ha) but they also say that if you don't find a job they will stop this benefit??? What the fuck ever happened to freedom of choice.

I clocked in and immediately tried to get into my work and ignore the uneducated morons that I work with. It's a harsh assumption but here are two examples of many. First break. I was sat reading Shakespeare when Frank walked up. Rugby player type and said 'Wot yer reading?'

'Shakespeare' says I.

'Fuckin' Shakespeare, why dunt ya read summat proper?'

Dinner break, Tony, bodybuilder, six foot two, telling me how he had shagged his babysitter five minutes before his wife came in and then proceeded to explain that if he caught her with anybody, he'd kill them both. Do you see what I'm up against? Turns out that later she ran off with another woman. (Poetic justice or what?)

I put up with the bullshit for the rest of the shift and with a degree of relief I was on my way home letting Andy's conversation go in one ear and out of the other.

Stepping through the front door at home I was confronted by our lass who had a look of laughable disbelief on her face.

'What's up with you?' I said.

'You're not gonna believe this' she said 'but we have had our dustbin nicked.'

'Eh?'

'Our dustbin. It's been nicked.'

I was incredulous.

'Was it full?'

'I don't know love but I've phoned the council and it's gonna cost sixty-four quid to replace.'

'Sixty-four fucking quid.' I was exasperated.

'And it's gonna take a week to replace.'

'Marvellous. I don't fucking believe this.'

'Me neither' she said 'but I've been talking to Sarah Jones today, y'know she sees that lad who's on heroin (which one I thought, there's fucking hundreds) and she's had three nicked, two were full as well.'

I wondered at this point if there was someone, somewhere who had a secret rubbish stash and was collecting it, but then all was revealed.

'She also said that what happens is that they nick the dustbins, empty them and then take them across the field to the Granada Service Station to the lorry park.'

This I could understand. They rolled the bins up to the lorry, slashed the curtain side of the wagon, threw the cargo inside the wheely bin and then legged it back, sometimes hotly pursued, back onto the estate. I wondered why they didn't use their own fucking bins. Is there anything thieves wouldn't nick? I doubted this.

'I can't afford sixty-four quid love.' I said.

'Me neither.'

I knew what had to be done. Now I'm no thief, but you've got to put your rubbish somewhere, so I would have to sink to their level, and engage in a covert operation and nick a dustbin. A fucking dustbin. I couldn't believe I was actually having to consider this, but what choice did I have? When in Rome.

I'd left it until late at night to do a quick reconnoitre under the guise of walking the dog with our lass. She having lived on the estate for years knew who lived where. I didn't want to be stealing some old dear's dustbin. As we walked around she sounded like she was singing the chorus from a corny song that she couldn't get out of her head. Single parent, thief, junky, miss a house. Single parent, thief, junky, miss a house, etc. After strolling around for an hour I had selected two targets. A fat ginger wanker called Jonny Jerkoff was one. A thief and small time dealer and the biggest shit stirrer I had ever known. I knew him from being in the same year at school. There was no love lost between us then as now. I didn't have a lot to do with him and it was tempting to get one back for all the grassing he'd done at school causing no slight interference to my truanting days.

The second choice was Jamie Burns. A young boy racer who I didn't mind at all and got on quite well with but I owed him for the time he'd belted the XR3i through the puddle I was walking past wetting me through. It delayed me going out on a Saturday night for an hour, which is no mean feat. I'd feel no guilt for taking off these people. I classed Jonny as a pay back and Jamie as just mischief.

With these targets selected it was time to put the plan into effect. It was Friday night so I felt safe with my assumption that the two target premises would be empty due to the occupier's being out on the piss. Jonny's was the first target as it was nearer. Approaching, I noticed that only the hall light was on. It was a good sign. I walked up as casual as anyone could who felt ridiculous about having to steal a dustbin. I quietly opened the gate and entered the garden. A quick furtive look around to make sure I wasn't being watched and I had my hands on the dustbin. Then I heard it. A low rumble. I looked around, senses alert. Nothing. I pulled the bin a couple of feet and heard it again along with the sound of a chain being dragged along the floor. Just as I realised what it was it was almost on top of me. The outhouse door had been cut away at the bottom to make a dog kennel. The coal-bunker blocked this from the view of the road. A big fucking German Shepherd came bounding at me, jaws agape and snapping, dragging a chain with it that must have once held the anchor to the Titanic. I felt like a cat must do. In one fluid movement I'd leapt back, spun round and was sprinting for the gate. I jumped and I'd almost cleared it when the searing pain of the dog's jaws clamping on my arse shot through my body holding me back just long enough for me to clip the top of the gate with my foot and land face first onto the pavement. I was in agony. I could feel the blood trickling down my arse cheek and thigh while the grazes on my face, hands, elbows and knees steadily stung. The dog was going ballistic at the gate trying to shove its head through the bars trying to get at me. I felt like booting the bastard but having a brain and not succumbing to emotions prevented this. The dog was only doing its job (marvellously).

It should get promotion. It's not the dog's fault but mine for not realising the fucking thing was there. With plan abandoned I ran away. I was in half a mind to go home but I wanted to get this over and done with. I headed for Jamie's, his car wasn't there. A good sign. I approached and checked for dogs, entered, grabbed the bin and left. I was paranoid at every sound of car engines. Jamie could pull round the corner and catch me red handed, or the Police even. I'd never live that down. In court for stealing a wheely bin. I wondered what the fine would be and had to laugh at the ridiculousness of the situation. I just couldn't believe I was pulling a stolen wheely bin through the estate. I couldn't decide whether to laugh or feel bad about being dragged down to someone else's level through no fault of my own. I entered our lass' garden and put the bin in the corner under the kitchen window. I got my bike lock and secured it to the drain pipe. I shook my head and thought, the things you've got to do sometimes.

Genitalia

He awoke to an annihilating headache. Tumble drier stomach. Joints so stiff and numb they felt as if they had been battered by a sadistic interrogator's cosh. The vile taste of sour beer polluted his mouth. Chemicals.

The curtains had been drawn wide-open and rare beams of TVland sunlight blazed into the room. He attempted to raise his hands to protect bloodshot eyes from the intruding, blinding lasers.

That was when he realised he was stark naked and manacled tightly to a wooden chair, with what appeared to be strong sinews of nylon washing line and dirt grafted skipping rope.

His first reaction was knee-jerk primeval. A vain, savage struggle to unleash himself from the restraints. Within seconds this approach was put paid to by that swirling stupor of potent hangover and the grievous cheese-wire tautness of the ropes. The man's perspiring brow slumped forward, his dehydrated well of strength exhausted. His torso palpitated, as if to vomit.

Five minutes of confused, anxious convalescence.

The man perceived with disdain that the ropes had somehow been bound to inflict painful friction burns on his ankles and wrists should any determined bid for freedom divulge itself.

A clock ticked. A ceaseless metronome of monotony. Somewhere in the distance a dog barked enthusiastically over a busy hum of traffic. Here, inside, a throbbing malaise harangued a disconcerted mind. His throat was as dry as desert sand.

He had been placed a metre or so from the window. Tentatively his comatose wits assimilated this knowledge and the man was shocked to discover, from the urban sprawl view, that he was a prisoner in his own ninth storey flat. Unease was stymied, slightly.

To resurrect his memory the man battled the day-after's waspish fuzz. What had happened the night before for him to wake in this predicament? Several pieces of jigsaw slotted together. He could recall meeting, at seven o'clock, the customary assortment of friends and acquaintances. Welcome, vivid pictures of public house carousing flickered across the screen of imagination like familiar scenes of a much viewed and loved silent movie. Later on, he had begun chasing vodka and the pristine sequence of events clouded into unfocused, random, vague, snatched stills. He had definitely entered the nightclub in the company of friends. Then. A blank. No matter how the man delved a revealing, untoward flashback would not manifest itself. There was nothing extraordinary.

He counted the seconds with the clock...seven...eight...nine...Then it hit him. The dark tunnel of ignorance was illuminated. He cursed. Who else but his damn mates? They had taxied him home and as a perverse, exuberant prank done this to him. With a tanked up, insensible victim it would have been easy. Right now, at his expense, the entire motley crew would be creased with laughter, tears streaming down their cheeks. Before they enjoyed breakfast at some truck stop cafe. Bastards. I'll kill them, the man vowed. All the same, with the puzzle solved and personal safety assured he afforded a heaving sigh of relief. Even the reassertion of forgotten headache did not quite seem so bad. Behind a rueful smile the man fantasised. An eye for an eye. The guillotine. The gallows. Well, perhaps not quite but the guilty culprits would suffer one way or...

'I see Rip Van Winkle's finally come round.' The man started abruptly. They were in the room. And they were a she. He remotely recognised the voice. From someplace. Where? 'Who the fuck are you?' He demanded, anger exacerbated by scorched skin the jolt to his system had incurred against the ropes. 'Fucking untie me will you? This isn't very funny.'

'Tut, tut. Such shameful language. Don't you remember me?' A saccharine whisper of gloating, victorious femininity.

'Should I? If you stood where I could see you it might help. Fucking untie me, will you?'

'In good time. Perhaps.'

'Look. Freak.' The man was almost hysterical. 'Yo! Ho! Ho! And a bottle of rum. You're a right laugh. But I've got a hangover and your joke has worn thin already. So fucking untie me. Whoever you are.'

'You seemed to remember me well enough last night.'

'Right now I can't remember last night. So just untie me!' A seizure of coughing was initiated by the man's zealous aggravation. A string of saliva dangled from his lips. He peevishly shook and spat it away. Behind him there was movement. He shuddered as a pair of sleek hands covered his eyes, blindman's bluff style. 'Guess who?' The voice was riddled with impertinent amusement.

'Well, you're not fucking Saint Nicholas, are you? Quit the horseplay. Just set me fucking free.'

'Speaking to a lady like that won't get you anywhere. Hasn't anyone ever told you that a lady loves to be flattered?'

'Fucking flattened, if you treat people like this. Untie me. Will you?'

'You were full of sweet talk last night.'

'It's morning now. What the hell is this about anyway? Will you fucking untie me? Now!'

'No.' Suddenly the voice lashed haughtily. The hands were withdrawn and the mystery female retreated. He strained, unsuccessfully, to catch a glimpse of his captor. 'I don't take orders from clowns who get themselves into foolish scrapes.' The tone was now a subzero snap.

The man's indignation became tempered by an inkling of trepidation. A bleak gust of fear swept through him, instigating another violent, infuriated endeavour to shake free of the bonds. The ropes implacably held firm; rubbing ever more harshly on the stinging sores of previous convulsions. Again he collapsed limp with defeat, panting and groaning. 'Oh fuck...I haven't done anything...what are you playing at?'

'You still don't remember, do you? You still haven't the foggiest idea who I am?'

He heard clodding tantrum stomps and then before his declining head a pair of smooth, slender pins. His neck craned and a hip-hugging skirt was revealed. Next, a pierced, toned navel. A skimpy black vest over small, pert breasts. Finally the enigma had a face.

'You! The girl from last week!'

SLAP!

Enraged, the man shook the effects of the blow away and stared with stubborn resolve into the combative countenance of the young woman. With an impetuous wave she flicked a straggle of hair from over her eyes.

'Is that all I was to you? The girl from last week. A one-night stand. A quick knee-trembler and bye-bye. You said you'd phone!'

'I was busy...'

'You were busy crawling round me, bevvied to the eyeballs, last night. You...You...You filthy scumbag!'

'That doesn't give you the right to bring me home, pissed up, and tie me up like you're some sort of serial killer. You crazy bitch!'

Their noses were almost touching.

'And you haven't the right to go round town on a Tuesday night telling every Tom, Dick and Harry what a shit screw I am. My workmates and bloody parents heard about it.'

She backtracked, flinching from a blast of fags and beer halitosis.

'So that's what this is all about. A few choice words in a bar and David Koresh is a stable human being by comparison.'

SLAP!

She had launched her full weight behind this second strike and the man floundered, pivoting between a conscious and unconscious state. As he recovered he judged, from the sound of clanking pottery, that she had stormed into the kitchen. His cheek burned unbearably and the need for paracetamol had magnified threefold.

A red mist threatened to swarm. But from somewhere a voice urged him to think. Think. Think. Calmer now, the man considered his options. Shouting for help would be practically useless. He lived in the flat at the end of a row. The only immediate neighbour was fast approaching eighty and wouldn't hear the opening salvoes of Armageddon if the forces of good and evil first locked horns in his bog. The occupants, whoever they were, of the flats above and below were seldom in. Besides, he didn't want this sordid little adventure to become a juicy joint for the local gossips to get their teeth into. By the time the fisherman got hold of the tale...The girl is hardly the secret love-child of Dr Goebbels and Myra Hindley, he reasoned. For the time being let her enjoy her joke. Try and play it cool he advised himself. And then.

He heard a cup being placed on the coffee table. She strode into his field of vision. It was a godsend to be met by a benign, almost remorseful smile as she drew the curtains tight shut.

'Thank fuck for that. The sunlight was slaughter.'

Attentively the woman rotated the man and chair in a half-circle, so that he faced the centre of the room. She sat in the armchair directly opposite the object of her game.

'You look funny, tied up, with no clothes on,' she quipped, teasing.

'Side-splitting I'm sure.'

'Nice place you'd have here if you weren't such a slob.'

'You said that last week.'

'You remember some things then. I see you've tidied up a little. Your CDs are all in the rack. Your magazines are on the shelf. There isn't soiled clothing littering the carpet, either. Were you expecting someone?'

'If you mean another woman, no. Are you going to end this madness?'

'When you've been put in your place. Maybe.' She pulled a silly face.

'For crying out loud. Get me a drink. An Alka-Seltzer. You might not have noticed but I'm not in the best of health.'

'Your manners are horrendous. Where are your Ps and Qs? This is all your own fault anyway. You shouldn't drink so much vodka. You shouldn't talk to strangers, either.' She grinned lavishly. He seethed at the exhibition of pleasure. Though he remained acutely aware that composure was paramount. 'Where are my manners? Thanks for tying me up. I'll send chocolates and flowers in future. We'll run off into the sunset and live happily ever after, shall we? Do you seriously hope to achieve anything by this?' He'd slaved like a navvy to swallow his humbled, smarting pride.

'What will I achieve? You tell me. What do you think this is about?'

'Without stating the blaring obvious I'd hazard a guess that you need medication and a shrink. What do you plan to do? Kill me? Come on, the party's over. Release me.'

'I wouldn't kill you...'

'That's a weight off my shoulders.'

'You're not worth a prison sentence.'

'You could go down for this. This amounts to kidnapping.'

'Oh, a well informed lawyer, isn't one?'

He covertly ground his teeth at the condescending tone.

'If I let you go, and if you went to the police, who do you think they'd believe? A man who was so plastered he couldn't remember his mother's maiden name or sweet innocent me.' She batted her eyelashes, an over-the-top Hollywood debutante. 'Sweet innocent me. Who'd had one too many and was brought home by wicked old you. The dirty beast that wanted to participate in a few dodgy sexual practices and...get the gist? Your word against mine. Anyhow, you wouldn't dare involve the police. Imagine how your mates would react if they got wind of this. You'd never live it down.' Her duplicity invigorated her. 'I've only tied you up. Plenty of men pay prostitutes to do that to them. Including a few Chiefs of Police, I shouldn't wonder.'

'That's a canny match. A whore and you. Look, just fucking untie me.' He yawned, demonstrably bored.

Volcano. The woman sprang to her feet, knocking the coffee table with her knee and splashing the contents of the mug messily over the hearthrug. He was wide-eyed to this eruption of impulse. 'You bastard. I'm no whore,' she remonstrated. 'You think you're God's gift, that's your problem. Mr Suave. We'll soon see how cool you are.'

Hell hath no fury like.

The man listened to the jangling of cutlery rashly swished around a drawer. In a flash she was towering over him. A pyre of domineering aplomb. Both hands were hidden behind her back. He had the disquieting intimation of shrinking into the chair. 'Still feel like King Don Juan, do we?'

146

'Possibly,' he replied with as much nonchalance as he could salvage. 'What are you hiding?' A trace of consternation slithered into his voice, despite his taking pains to repress it.

'Scissors.' Her blue orbs glimmered. The glee of an unrepentant sinner. 'You haven't had breakfast yet, so it's time to snip a link of sausage.' She exposed the shining implements.

'Oh no!' He rocked the chair backwards onto its hind legs, as far away from her as he could get. 'You can't! Don't! Don't!'

On her knees she began to tease. Tantalisingly she stroked a palm down the man's chest. Whispering crude sweet nothings. Down she went. Lingering in the hairs of his belly. Down. Downwards. Ever down. In deliberate rapturous circles. Her hand rested on his cock.

'No! No! You can't! Don't! Fucking arrrggghhh!'

'It wasn't floppy like this before.' She placed the man's phallus between the blades of steel.

The colour drained from his cheeks. His eyes watered. His heart raced. His throat constricted. She squeezed the handles torturously together. Until he could feel the nightmare. Sharp, cold steel nipping and biting into the flesh of his treasured appendage. She held the scissors firm, never wavering. 'Would Sir like a trim?' She smirked.

He experienced pre-death rigor mortis. He tried to beg for mercy but heard only the pounding of pulse against eardrums. He tried to plead forgiveness. He was a village idiot mute. She gazed deep into saucer pupils.

An immense exertion. 'P-p-please.' A diminutive guttural sob of a little boy lost. 'Please.' Helium pitched appeal.

'That's more like it. I love it when you're polite.'

'P-p-please move the scissors a-a-away.'

The grip of the scissors was relaxed. The woman stood for a brief instant, gratified by his submission. Then she reclaimed her seat like a monarch taking the throne. She was aglow with satisfaction. 'It's true then. A man really does think with his knob.'

He sat like a sculptured witness to death-camp atrocities. She waited for the trauma to diminish.

Eventually, in matter of fact cadences, she spoke. 'I really liked you. I stayed in every night waiting for you to phone like you said you would. To rub salt in the sores one of my bitchy workmates spent an evening in the pub. The cow was over the moon to hear about our inglorious sexapade. There are rumours flying left, right and centre about me at work. People think I'm a slut. I don't do one night stands. You were the first and you're going to be the last. I've slept with very few men.'

He was as solemn as a suicide inquest. 'How was I to know that you were like that? Or felt like that? It's not like I raped you. It was a bit of harmless fun. It was harmless until you nearly chopped my dick off. Please, untie me now. How would you like this treatment?'

'Not very much, I admit. There again I didn't like you telling all and sundry that I'm useless in bed. I'm not that bad am I?'

'No,' the man replied contritely. 'I was showing off I suppose.' In reality he had been so whacked by skunk and beer on the night of their lover's embrace he could scarcely remember the act. He had concocted a story to satisfy the lecherous curiosity of the pub's clientele.

'You show off quite a bit. You're showing off all you've got now.' She giggled. 'I'll bet there's plenty endowed with more. That said, you do look fetching in a weird kind of way. All vulnerable. When you're sloshed you're all over me.' She pouted.

'Enough is enough. Please.'

She blew a kiss. He blew a frustrated sigh. She blew another, more erotic kiss. Let. Me. Go. She rose. Gradually. Provocatively. Spellbinding. Her hands caressed her inner thighs. In slow motion. Her lithe fingers ascended. With lust. Sensuous touch. Insatiable. Vanishing beneath her skirt. Speculatively. He hung from tenterhooks. Butterflies of arousal. Alarm bells of caution. She peeled her knickers down. Saucy smile. Striptease cancan. Kicked away her panties. She lifted her clothing. Flashing. A mound of dark velvety hair.

'I think this is what you wanted.' Puckered lips. 'Do you still want it?'

'For god's sake.' Apprehension.

She lap danced. Closer. Salaciously wiggling. Writhing. Ecstatically. Thumping heartbeat. She was over him. So close. The musky aroma. Her sex.

'Gagging for it.'

'Fucking untie me.' Panic. More devilry unfolding.

'Do you want it?' A disco diva. In a brothel.

Laughter. A firm hand in his mop of hair. Gyrating genitalia. In a gobsmacked mush. A recalcitrant daughter. 'You can have it.' On a mission of parent baiting. Mischief. 'You want it?' Feisty. Flamboyant shake of hips. A push of rebuke.

She broke the spell. The seat toppled backwards and banged hard against the floor. The man moaned; impact of the crash buffered by his shoulder blades. 'You can have it. You poor, poor thing,' she goaded, splaying one leg either side of his grimace.

The woman proceeded to urinate. He gasped outraged as a hot golden waterfall cascaded from her Garden of Eden. The stream of piss bubbled and gurgled over his features.

Having spent her penny she caricatured a great philosopher, hand on chin, objectively contemplating her subject. Pacified, she restored her modesty. Systematically. The show was over. 'Did you like that?' She tested the audience's approval, blushing a blood red hue.

'You're fucking loco,' the man blurted, odious droplets dribbling from his lips. 'It's fucking everywhere. It's burning my eyes. Get a cloth. Get it out of my face. Jesus Christ.'

He thought her laughter resembled the hag-like croaking of a witch. She was too overcome with hilarity to think anything.

Nevertheless the woman soon emerged from the bathroom with two, dry clean towels. After hoisting the man and chair into an upright posture she wiped the miasmic liquid away. She used the second towel as an ad hoc gag and mutterings of dissent were silenced.

'You slept late. It's dinnertime and I'm famished. We don't want you screaming for help if an unannounced visitor knocks on the door, do we?'

At long last she treated him to a pint of cool water. He guzzled with the thirst of a castaway at an oasis. She didn't spill a drop. She held a cigarette to his mouth. He inhaled intense steady drags; a man who had fantastically survived a firing squad.

They sat watching TV. For their mutual entertainment she had chosen a nineteen sixties monochrome thriller. He hated BBC2 on a

Saturday afternoon. Villain gets caught. Hero gets plaudits. Girl gets hero. He silently likened it to premature euthanasia.

'You didn't have much in the freezer,' the woman complained but without tetchiness. She tucked into the plate of southern fried chicken and chips that nestled on her lap. 'Are you positive you don't want any?'

Blankly the man declined the proffered forkful of chicken.

'Do you think this film will be any good? How much of this do you think I've missed?'

Without awaiting a reply she picked up the remote control, summoned Ceefax and keyed in the appropriate listings page. 'Oh, it only started fifteen minutes ago,' happily acknowledging the screened information. 'I haven't heard of any of the actors,' she added as a suspicious afterthought.

Again the man asked to be released. The woman ignored the request. Her undivided attention the sole property of the incorrigible villain of the celluloid drama. She viewed with pursed lips. As the dangerously handsome criminal forced, at gunpoint, the dumb but beautiful leading lady into the boot of a stereotypically black, sinister automobile.

'They're all the same these films, like men.' She criticised succinctly.

'Most men aren't roped to a chair. Prisoners in their own home,' he countered, riled. 'Now be sensible.'

'I don't feel like it, I'm busy. If you hadn't been so awful when you woke up I'd have let you go ages ago. You reap what you sow.' Her eyes didn't stray from the motion picture. The crook was penning a ransom note. The man prayed that the film didn't give the woman grandiose ideas.

'Tell me why you didn't phone. Didn't you fancy me after you'd had me?'

'Do we have to go round in ever decreasing circles? Look, we all suffer rejection...'

Her head swivelled sharply.

'...You can't imprison people just because they don't give you a fucking bell. I could end up losing the use of a limb these ropes are so tight. Seriously.'

'So you rejected me.'

'I don't know,' he answered hastily diplomatic. 'And I'm sorry that I spread nasty stories. It was childish. But believe me I don't half fucking regret it now. Please untie me.' So I can string you up.

'You're like a parrot. And I wish you wouldn't swear so much. It's cheap.'

Even so he was certain his penitence had touched on a sympathetic nerve.

'Another thing, where the hell did you learn to fasten knots like this?'

'I go abseiling and rock-climbing in the dales,' she replied, distracted.

She ate in a meditative trance. He would have amicably commented that he could hear the workings of her mind ticking over. If it wasn't for the ropes. If it wasn't for the humiliation of being pissed over. If the memory of his knob in the jaws of a pair of scissors didn't send hypothermic shivers along his spine.

This has gone way too far, the man acrimoniously mused, as the splashes and slurps of washing up emanated from the kitchen. He would have to tolerate the scandal. He was going to the law. Or he'd break her neck when she undid the shackles. He preferred the latter.

When she took the vacuum from the lobby he was petrified by a fleeting, hellish hallucination of various suction pipes inflicting unspeakable damage on a particularly cherished piece of his anatomy. She began vacuuming the living room.

Conversationally she told him that when she was a child she had always longed to own a horse. Her dream had never been realised, but she had compensated by recently paying a local artist to paint for her a picture of a chestnut mare. The picture took pride of place in her own living room. Without insolance he said that he had no interest in horses, he only bet on the outcome of football matches.

After vacuuming the bedroom and mopping the kitchen floor she further confided that she would like to spend six months back-packing throughout Asia. He couldn't cope with that but wouldn't mind a debauched weekend in Amsterdam. She turned up her nose, disapprovingly.

The drone of a washing machine jumbling into action rekindled recognition of his self-inflicted alcohol malady. Although he had recuperated quite substantially by now. 'I've even put your dirty underwear in,' she said like Mother Theresa blessing an Aids victim.

She polished the windows. She dusted the mantelpiece. And fastidiously gleamed each individual miscellaneous plastic gadget that cared to masquerade as an ornament. 'Star Wars is for boys not men,' she instructed, locating a spick and span figurine of Han Solo next to the CD player. She observed, with houseproud chagrin, that it was the first time the place had seen Mister Sheen for months. He gawped at her dumbfounded.

Meticulously hanging the clean laundry in the airing cupboard she expressed, through the walls, an ambition to work with animals. He sarcastically declared that he presently did a passable impersonation of a chimpanzee at the vivisectionists. She knew that, she said, nonplussed.

He had given up all hope of an early pardon. So they talked some more. Small talk. Disagreeing over every infinitesimal irrelevant detail in the process. It went on for two hours.

She told him he was stupid. In his delicate, dubious position he should have agreed to everything she said. Had she been a raving lunatic, she explained, she wouldn't have taken too kindly to his attitude. What if she had thought he had only been saying yes to gain her confidence? He asked. She wouldn't have taken too kindly to that, either, had she been a raving lunatic. 'You can't win with raving lunatics,' he commented dryly. 'Will you release me?'

'No.'

'See what I mean?'

'You like your jokes, don't you?'

For the benefit of the constable heading inquiries the man made a mental note that it was just before five o'clock when the woman began slipping into her coat. She made herself presentable in the mirror and proclaimed jubilantly, 'I'm going. I heard your friends say they'd call around six. I'll leave the door unlocked for them.'

She found it difficult to disguise her exhilaration at his beseeching, anguished expression of abandonment and injustice.

In the doorway between the living room and the hall she paused, clicked her tongue and finally concluded, 'don't call me, I'll call you.' The man heard the outer door close.

Then she was gone.

Supermarket

Supermarket. Out here, on the front line, in the store, life goes on unaware of the dishonourable dealings behind the scenes. Special offer soups and somnolent shoppers.

Little Tommy Burns, aged eight, didn't want to come here. Still, it's better than school he tries to kid himself. There are second thoughts. The boy is too honest for his own good. Teachers tell you off, mothers tell you off, wherever and whenever something interesting is happening.

Little Tommy has been to the dentist and has had two fillings. He didn't complain or cry while the dentist messed about in his mouth with a thing that, Tommy thought, looked and sounded like an alien laser gun. If Tommy had been the dentist he would have picked that big bogey from up that hairy nostril before zapping anyone's teeth.

Little Tommy's mother was ever so proud of her son's bravery and all-round behaviour. Leaving the surgery she promised to buy the boy a treat if he was just as good in the supermarket. Tommy considered that he had been just as good, despite wiping one of his own bogeys on a bunch of bananas in a basket. If dentists are allowed to have bogeys then he, little Tommy, should be allowed to have bogeys and do whatever he liked with them, the boy reasoned. All the same he made sure he had picked his nose while his mother looked away, inspecting the ripeness of tomatoes.

Little Tommy wondered if dentists really are aliens. Aliens that control people with a special power, gradually turning them into slaves. All the grown-ups here looked like they were under an alien power's command, like sometimes you see on Saturday morning cartoons. Tommy wasn't exactly bothered by this speculation. More quietly confident that if alien invaders were on the loose he would be able to save the world.

Supermarkets are rubbish and boring Tommy thought. 'Mum, Mum, can we go home now? Can we? Can we?'

'We won't be long now, darling. Remember if you keep on being good I'll buy you something nice.' Tommy thought he would like a water gun he had seen in Woolworths, just in case an alien invasion really was imminent.

Tommy pulled a face at a man who appeared equally as bored, pushing the trolley for his wife. The man pulled a face back. Tommy was pleased. That man will help fight the aliens if a spaceship is on its way to take over the earth.

Old Tommy West, aged seventy-six, didn't want to be here. Normally he shopped on a Saturday, first thing. But tomorrow was a special day. Old Tommy was going on a trip to the coast with the other old fellow's who lived at the home. Something to look forward to for once. Halves of bitter, sea air, fish 'n' chips, mussels. It would do his chest good.

Old Tommy grumbled at the prices. Bloody con-artists. Things were never like this in his day. Without gloomy sentiment old Tommy often thought that he was glad he was coming to the end of his life. He'd had a good one and he didn't like all this newfangled junk that cluttered the world. Almost ready to find out what really is on the other side of the big mystery despite still being reasonably well in body and still very sharp in mind. Get the social trip over and done with, another few years watching and waiting and then Bob's your uncle, my time will be up, the old man daydreamed. He placed a tin of Irish stew into his basket knowing full well it wouldn't be nearly so wholesome and tasty as that his grandmother used to cook. All those years ago.

'I've been to the dentist.' A young boy spoke.

Old Tommy looked down. 'What did he do?'

'Not sure.'

Little Tommy didn't want to say too much in case the old man was an alien saboteur.

'I'll bet you eat too many sweets.'

Little Tommy screwed up his face, becoming suspicious and tight-lipped. That wart on the old man's chin might carry tiny aliens around. When the wart burst and the aliens popped out they might grow into monsters the size of houses.

Old Tommy knew a thing or two about kids, being the father of seven he now no longer saw. Gramps stuck up his thumb, stuck out his tongue and the boy's doubts were somehow magically allayed. The young boy answered the old man. 'That's what my mum said, that I eat too many sweets, I mean. Do you like supermarkets?'

'No.' The old man laughed, phelgm rattling on his chest and in his throat.

'I hate supermarkets. You smoke too much.'

'I suppose I do.' Still smiling old Tommy rummaged in his pocket and produced a couple of green mints. 'A couple more won't make them all fall out.'

'What do you say?' Said Tommy's mum, returning the old man's smile.

'Thank you.'

'Be a good boy for your mum.'

The mother, the son and the old man part company.

Of Those Who Live
In the Shadows

'Iyeard't sound una sleeper one night, a martyr ooze screams'd echoed int livin' room fur over twenty years. Id bin treer nailed tut wall. Y'could smell 'is blood as it ran down't wall from his wrists.

'A felt 'is last breath, it med ripples int air.'

Forty-seven Hellfield Road was an old townhouse, built in the early twentieth century, the gable end of a short terrace. It sat adjacent to the local high school and the facing gable end was a fine public house. Horsechestnut trees softened the glare of the sun in the summer yet allowed enough light to give the place an airy feel. From outside the flats looked quite run-down. The paint on the external doors and window frames had started peeling and school children had written their names in marker pen, all over the walls. The bay window was starting to rot and one of the panes of glass had cracked, the front garden was a thin layer of pebbles with one plate, a holly bush, which had probably grown from a cutting some past tenant had planted after Christmas one year.

'Wi shoulda follered us instincts. Wi sawt place an laughed ut how grim it looked. Widdint look ut any other flats, wi just went for it like it sucked us in or summat.'

In the late sixties and early seventies the owner of the house was a practitioner of the black arts, a man known only as the Buglar of Buglar 6. Forty-seven Hellfield Road was his laboratory. He had marked his territory by painting the inside walls with blood and urine, a process which took nearly two years.

The Buglar had a reputation among locals as an odd and dangerous man, the sort of man mothers would warn their children about. The sort of man who attracted the attention of children who would walk by that way just to see the 'spook house'.

'The house creaked at night, especially if yu went tu bed 'n noticed yud left a light on.'

The Buglar died in the mid-seventies. Police eventually entered the house after neighbours had complained about the smell. The officers who found the body reported finding the mutilated bodies of nine men. The Buglar was said to have a smile on his face.

From diaries left by the Buglar it was said that he had been attempting to open a gateway to hell.

'Iyad a dream one night, thuwarra blasta light int flat unna scream, an evil scream, summat breathed out and exploded, sealing a huge hole where darkness poured out. Wax ran downt walls, I felt a tingle us calm set in.

'Evil lurked int shadders, demons projected into the walls, light moved in dark like a TV screen int corners unt rooms, wax stopped int walls an yukked see things movin int dark at night.'

The local area was quite industrialised, malt kilns, scrap yards, chemical and chocolate manufacture, gardens etc. A graveyard was broken into two by Hellfield Road, that wasn't the resting place of the Buglar.

The house had been converted into flats in the eighties, a victim of the reclaimers.

'Iyadtu deal wi Missus Lobstervine whenever owt went wrong wit flat. She were't sorta person who were fine tu yur face but 'er eyes never flinched. Shid seem reight good 'n understandin but shi never did oat about repairs. 'Somebodt'll come tu fix it' she always sed.'

LESSONS OF THE MODERN WORLD No. 1
Estate agents are crooks.

See how simple this statement is, there are several alternative versions which may be used - estate agents are scum, estate agents are bent bastards and should never be trusted etc. For five pounds an hour, you can sell your soul to the devil but you can pay two hundred and fifty pounds a month for him to fuck you up the arse.

164

'Afelt like a lived wit earthworms, it started raining, two weeks it pissed it down, non-stop. T'earthworms wur forced tu commit suicide, thur bodies ud get clots undet skinun thud riggle reight tence like. Thur were better off dead, dyin slow than livin under hell.'

NOVEMBER20th 2000.
I cried as I rose from earth
Death all around
Small, pale bodied
As rain came down
They drowned
I cleansed
My tears, both of sadness
And of joy

The last tenants of forty-seven Hellfield Road were lucky to be able to heal themselves with the powerful energies of Reiki and crystals.

The earthworms died and were lost amongst the autumnal leaves which scattered the pavement outside.

Simon had to remain centered even though life had become chaotic, each day would bring new tests of strength. The baywindow had started to leak, black mould spores grew on the walls in each room, rising and penetrating damp raised it's ugly head.

The gas fire in the living room came away from the wall, the light switch in the kitchen was unsafe due to dampness surrounding it.

'Miyangel tore er wings 'n broke er halo as she fell frumt sky 'n banged er hed ont bathroom sinkon er way down.'

The world is a tough place for one so innocent as an angel.

Simon tried cleansing the flat when they moved in by placing quartz crystals in the windows, the place was buzzing with bad magic.

He'd been punished for his sins in the past, misery and pain had ruled his life but now he was truly happy, in love and in harmony with his life. He'd actually grown to love himself, something which would have previously been unthinkable.

A serpent of industrial noise swam outside in the cold, November air. The stench of Castleford and malt vinegar hung on his breath.

Simon and his angel were warm in bed, sleeping, uneasily. The bay window threatened to collapse in tears.

December started and with the start of a new month came new happiness, sunshine and clear skies.

Forty seven Hellfield Road was emptied on the second, a Saturday, the property had been condemned by environmental health, the officer who condemned the place had smelled the mould on entering and had then gone on to notice the lack of adjoining fire alarms, fire doors, rising and penetrating damp and a general state of disrepair worthy of the place's fate. No-one was to live in either of the flats until all repairs had being carried out.

Simon awoke the morning after, painted blue with Lapis Lazuli, surrounded by love in a beautifully maintained, four bedroom terrace house in Normanton.

'Medicine man, doctor sie in the sky.'
Of those who live in shadows
the one I love most I'm with
Count blessings daily
Comforted by a guide
Buddha sits gracefully
a living room for two
shine bright in the northern sky
clearly mark our path
Of those who live in shadows
We believe in our strength
a complete circle
our worlds the same
I see through your eyes
Healing immaculate
one

Kip

Kip didn't immediately recognise the room he had awoken in but, then again, he could hardly see past his hangover. Gazing upon the gaudy green wallpaper and sniffing in the musty smell, it took a couple of seconds to sink in, but he soon realised he was in Brent's flat. The alarm bells started ringing.

Brent was a mate, but being in his flat meant that Kip wasn't at home with his wife Denise as he should be. He couldn't remember if he had phoned her the night before to let her know where he was. A couple of secondary concerns crept and meandered their way casually past his headache and general grogginess. Was he late for work? He glanced around but couldn't see a clock. More importantly, where was his car to get him there? It was a standing rule with Kip, no drink driving, well not pissed anyway. He quickly figured out that with him being at Brent's meant he must have left his car somewhere else. Judging by his hangover he knew he'd been well pissed.

The couple of drinks with the lads after work had metamorphosised into an epic piss-up. It was only coming back to him slowly.

He rubbed his hands over his face and stared at the ceiling through his fingers and thought to himself that he couldn't face the day. He then swung himself upright and told himself he might as well have a go anyway.

After a brief search he found his coat on the kitchen floor and took out his mobile. He worked out he had forty-five minutes to discover where his car was and get to work on time. Saturday mornings were not generally his forte when it came to punctuality and another bollocking from the area manager didn't seem too appealing. He punched his home phone number into the keypad, simultaneously drinking copious amounts of water and noticing the food stains down the front of his shirt and trousers. This would mean having to go home to get changed which he was hoping to avoid because he'd rather go straight to work as he didn't fancy facing Denise with a hangover. But you couldn't be a Hoover salesman and expect to sell any Hoovers with the previous night's Chinese all down your front. Not if you wanted or, more specifically, needed the sales bonus. Kip contemplated borrowing some of Brent's clothes but dismissed the idea. Brent was slightly bigger build than Kip and the baggy look just wasn't in at the moment. Strictly taboo in fact.

The phone connected and he heard Denise say 'hello'. Just by her tone he knew he was in the shit. His subtle pacifying words were met with silence, followed by the dialling tone as she hung up. He hated it when she did that.

It was the seventh call to local bars, he tried every one that he could possibly have been to. He could hear a cleaner clattering a mop and bucket at the other end of the line when a man's gruff voice confirmed his car was in the car park of The Tap and Barrel. Another two calls and a girl at the taxi rank said there'd be a car there in ten minutes. Kip left Brent's flat leaving the door on the latch. He stood and watched an empty crisp packet blow across the tarmac on a slight breeze because it was the only activity to watch. He played with his mobile idly and bored with that his thoughts drifted back to Denise and the argument and accusations that would be forthcoming. The taxi pulled up (seven minutes late he noticed) and broke his thoughts. He opened the door and climbed in.

'The Tap and Barrel on Finkle Street,' replied Kip.

The cabbie tried small talk with Kip who wasn't in the mood. The driver reminded him of Gordon, a cabbie from his hometown. He hoped his driver's demeanour was different because Gordon had once delighted in telling Kip how if attractive young pissed-up girls were short of their taxi fare he would intimidate and threaten to take them to the police for prosecution, sometimes driving towards the police station unless some compromise, generally sexual, could be arranged. He said it usually worked on naïve young minds. Kip seriously hoped that Gordon was merely an abnormal type of perverted individual, but drew parallels with the lads he knew of who dropped pills into girls' drinks to make sure there were no inhibitions when it came to getting into their knickers. He couldn't understand what was wrong with these people. Were they unable to converse? Hindered romantically? Too ugly to stand a chance under normal circumstances? Or just too selfish to consider or grasp another person's emotions? Maybe them all. It seemed to Kip they wanted to manipulate emotions not understand them. It's an urban jungle out there Kip thought, and the prospect of his daughter Bethany growing up with leeches like that around made him shudder. His phone rang interrupting these dark thoughts.

It was Mark, Kip's manager, this was unusual for a Saturday.

'Morning Kip.' Enthusiastic.

'Alright Mark what's up?' said Kip guardedly.

'Nothing much, it's just there's two new starters on the books today. I said I'd pick them up and take them on the rounds, but head-office want me there. I was wondering if you'd mind picking them up and taking them with you? Show them the ropes.'

Kip's mind was ticking over quickly, if Mark was going through to head-office it meant that he wouldn't be at work when Kip arrived. Glancing at the clock on the dashboard Kip knew almost certainly he was going to be late. Simple.

'Who are they and where do I pick them up?'

'Raheal a Pakistani lad, he's into cricket big time apparently.'

Boring thought Kip, having absolutely no interest in the subject whatsoever.

'And Kerry a nineteen year old student.'

Really. Kippers imagination was already on the last statement. This could put a different edge on the outlook of his day.

'Pick them up at work will you, 10 o'clock. Sure you don't mind?'

'No, it's no problem at all, you know me Mark, I'm a company man.'

Tell him what he wants to hear, Kip theorised.

'Good man, see you Monday.'

Kipper paid a begrudging and what he classed as extortionate six quid, told the driver he'd been a fucking right laugh and got out. He caught sight of his car. Kipper really liked his car. He'd wanted one from being seventeen, a Golf GTI in tornado red, BBS alloys, Goodmans six-speaker stereo system, jet-black interior and jan speed exhaust. He'd just spent four hundred, which he could ill afford, on new big end bearings and having the heads skimmed, giving it an extra 12 BHP and taking it to one hundred and thirty-seven miles per hour. If Denise ever found out about this she'd kill him. Literally.

As he sat and closed the door he relaxed a little. Composing himself as he knew at this point he'd still almost certainly be over the drink-driving limit. He savoured the smell of the interior, the fabric, the air freshener and plastic before inserting the key. Turning on the ignition Bon Jovi exploded in a wall of sound scaring Kip half to death.

He was pushing ninety-five down the motorway, his window down, arm hanging out loosely, listening to the drawn out windrush of passing traffic and his Bon Jovi tape. He'd formulated the plan of picking Kerry and Raheal up first and then calling at home to get changed and face the music from Denise. It would be quicker that way as it was a circuitous route. At ninety-five it didn't take long before he was pulling into the car park of his employers.

Raheal and Kerry had already been waiting for a quarter of an hour and were sharing another uncomfortable silence as the preliminary courtesies and short polite conversations had ground to a halt again. Kerry was convinced that Raheal was flirting, Raheal thought she had a fit body but wasn't much to look at, when Kip arrived.

'Raheal and Kerry is it?' asked Kip.

They both looked at each other and then back at Kip, nodding in unison. They didn't quite know what to think. There was a guy stood in front of them stinking of stale beer and looking like he'd been run over by a pizza delivery. He explained that he was their boss for the day and would they mind waiting in the car for two minutes while he collected his rota. They duly obliged.

Kip went to the office and walked over to Mark's desk, noticing

Kerry out of the office window, crouching, getting into the car. He moved a half full ashtray that was doubling as a paperweight and collected his rota from an untidy pile of papers. Only three houses to visit, he might be done for mid-afternoon he speculated and headed for the GTI.

Kip briefed his new colleagues on route to his house about what the job entailed and also explained his predicament. He was glad when they were amiable about calling to his house first. It was strictly against company policy and he sincerely hoped Raheal and Kerry could keep secrets so it didn't get back to Mark. But he felt they were getting along alright, not at all what he first expected. They'd both been out the night before and had slight hangovers themselves. They've got a pretty laid back attitude, Kip was reasoning. A short while later they were bursting into laughter, swapping tales of drunkenness and stupidity from the night before, taking the piss out of each other light-heartedly when the opportunity arose, good-natured banter.

Denise was at the front bay window cuddling Bethany close to her chest. As she saw him step out of the car she turned and walked out of view. Kerry was embarrassed. The uproar that was coming from inside the house, the couple shouting at each other above the baby screaming, the crashes, the slamming and banging of doors and profanity of language being hurled had set the neighbour's nets twitching and inspired the old man from next door, one who never walked the dog, to peel his armchair from the skinny contours of his body and find the dog's lead. He sauntered past the car having sneaky cursory sideways glances at the occupants, then half turning, on the pretence of calling his dog, turned his attention and took numerous covert prying glances at the offending house.

Raheal wasn't particularly bothered about the people, some were standing at their gates by now watching the debacle. You couldn't grow up being Asian on an all white council estate and not get used to folk staring. With a curt 'fuck you' directed into the house Kip emerged from the front door slamming it shut behind him. The neighbours diverted their eyes elsewhere and comments shifted to last night's Coronation Street and elsewhere an old man with his dog disappeared around a corner.

Storming up to the car Kip was trying to collate his feelings, to regain a little composure but still slammed the car door, rammed into gear and sped away in a screech of tyres and smoke oblivious to the tut tuts and shaking of heads from neighbours.

Raheal and Kerry could feel the tension emanating from him so with tentative awkwardness Raheal took it upon himself to lighten the mood.

'You alright mate?'

'Yeah,' said Kip 'it's just a domestic argument.'

'Sounded like a fucking war to me,' said Raheal with half a laugh and a smile, but felt uncomfortable when Kip just checked his rear view mirror and offered no reply.

Kerry sensed it was her turn to try to sway the tide.

'Can I ask you a question Kip?'

'Sure.'

'How did you get your name, I mean, were you christened Kip, is it a nickname or short for something?'

'It's short for Kipper.'

'Kipper?'

'Yeah, my Christian name is Christopher, but when I was young I pronounced Christopher as Kipifer which in turn got distorted to Kipper then shortened to Kip.'

Kerry laughed to herself but could tell by the way Kip turned on the stereo and concentrated on his driving that his mind was elsewhere.

'That was a classic example of a salesman's manipulative charms at their finest. Three appointments obligated and three hoovers sold. Piece of piss. I told you they practically sold themselves didn't I?' Kip was jubilantly clapping his hands and rubbing his palms together as they made their way to the car. But the row that morning was still lingering, festering like a cancerous growth at the back of his mind, almost contained, nearly subdued but tarnishing what should have been a good mood for him. Maybe a couple of drinks with his new colleagues would help, besides that, it would show Denise that he was his own man and if he wanted a drink, he'd go for one. What was the point, anyway, in going straight home like a sorrowful puppy to sit in a bad atmosphere and cold silence? Fuck it he thought.

'Do you fancy coming for a couple of celebratory drinks now that we've finished, it's my treat…'

It wasn't until his fifth pint of Stella had been quaffed and the atrocious shot at pool had been played that Kip realised he was looking through eyes that had taken on an iridescent texture. He was pissed. If it wasn't for the fact that Raheal had offered to drive the car after many hints (he'd passed his test but didn't own a car and oh how fucking cool is your GTI kind of business) plus the fact that Kip was in an amiable mood, he would have stuck to the original plan of just a couple of pints. So as the black ball was sunk and he'd handed a fiver to Kerry, who'd won, he decided it was about the right time to leave.

'I can't believe you've won I'm quite surprised at that Kerry,' he managed to say with just the hint of slur.

'I grew up in a pub,' she explained.

'Hustler.'

She laughed as they left.

It felt strange to Kip to be sitting in the passenger seat of his own car, but he was relaxed and enjoying the ride.

'If you take the next right there's a long stretch of road where you can open her up and see what she's capable of,' Kip offered.

'Sound. She's beauty to drive.' An excited Raheal was commenting as he took the right turn with a slight screech of tyres.

'Easy,' said Kip.

'It's okay' said Raheal 'I'm getting used to the handling now' as he pushed harder on the accelerator and watched the speedometer push its way clockwise.

Kerry sat in the backseat unimpressed by the conversation. Typical lads on a car and testosterone rush.

'I'll put some music on. I've got just the song to accentuate the moment.'

Raheal's eyes were wide as he glanced at the speedo and then back to the road. He was just pushing one hundred and thirty as Kip announced he'd found the song he wanted. He sat back just in time to see the sharp left bend looming up on them far too fast. Kerry screamed a shrill shriek as the realisation of the situation hit her. Kip had never heard a sound like it and as Raheal's eyes met the road from the speedo he too knew it was too late. His automatic reactions of slamming the brakes on and trying to take the bend were to no avail. The car skidded sideways, screeching, smoke billowing from the tyres as the car's off side wheels struck the kerb, forcing the tyres to relinquish their grip and flipping it, turning it over sideways through mid air. Inside the moments rode so slowly upon one another, exhausted before they fell upon the next. This is where death lurked close to life.

The car hit the fallow field about sixty meters from the take off point, crumpling it, shattering windows, spinning it over and over until eventually it came to a stop in a crumpled heap of metal, blood and steam.

It was the brightness of light and the noise that interrupted the unconsciousness that had enveloped Kip. The sterile smell also hit him as his eyes flickered open and through a blurred vision he started to focus first on the hospital room and then Denise. Tears were streaming down her face from puffed up red eyes. What had happened slowly came back to Kip as his head pounded and body ached. His own tears started to flow. Denise moved to the bed and gently held Kip. He put his arms around her in automatic response and felt a flood of warm emotion. The weight of her body hurt his battered frame but it didn't matter, Denise is what did.

'I thought I'd lost you Kip. The doctors say you were lucky. And I couldn't have lived with myself if anything had. With the row and everything. I'm so sorry and I never want to do it again.'

'Shh it's alright love,' was the only thing Kip's numbed mind could offer 'what about the other two?'

'They've been discharged, shock, slight concussion and cuts and bruises. Same as you but your concussion was worse, you've been unconscious for hours. They want to keep you in for a couple of days. The police said they couldn't believe anyone had survived.'

She burst into tears again.

As he lay there his own eyes welling up he was reflecting on what he'd just been told. The doctors said he was lucky. He didn't feel it. He figured he was an unlucky victim of bad emotions and circumstance. As they both lay there he was trying to work out how you can be lucky and unlucky at the same time.

Carpet Burns

'I should never have started seeing you! All my friends warned me, they could see exactly what you're like, see straight through you - and now I can too! You don't care about anybody or anything else so long as you're all right, Jack. Nothing but a selfish moron.'

'And you're nothing but a Mrs Mop two decades before your time. You'll be wearing wrinkled stockings next. As for your friends, do you seriously think I give a monkey's chuff about them? Or what they think?'

She stormed into the kitchen: a tempest of manic mutterings, slammed cupboard doors, quick-fire obscenities. Then a plate crashed to the floor. A scream! Venomous though oddly futile - wailing over broken pottery like crying over spilt milk. Serves her right, he sneered. The volume of her curses rose as she swept jagged fragments onto a dustpan and dumped them into the bin. And more sniping rolled from her tongue as she rumbled back into the living room. 'I'm sick of the sight of you if you want to know the truth!'

'And I'm sick of hearing you - nagging about one thing and then another. I suppose you'll try blaming me for the plate you've just broken next. Will you ever learn to keep your big complaining mouth shut? At least some of the time?'

'I've a big mouth? Try listening to yourself sometime. And yes, if you weren't so argumentative I wouldn't have been in such a tizz when I picked the plate up and therefore probably wouldn't have dropped it.'

'You'd try talking your way out of a murder charge if they caught you with a bloodstained knife in your hand.'

'If I live with you much longer they probably will find me with a bloodstained knife in my hand.'

'And if I live with you much longer someone will probably nominate me for a fucking Nobel Peace Prize. You'll swear black is white and white is not the colour of snow. You either need your eyes testing or a lobotomy, I'm not sure which.'

'I've really had about as much as I can take from you. Out! Out of my home! I want you out!'

'I pay as much rent as you, why don't you get lost?'

'Because the rent book has my name on it. You are - or were - my guest. Now get out!' She grabbed the denim jacket from over the back of the armchair he was sat in and flung it to the floor, as if it symbolised something deeply offensive or useless, refuse to be discarded now rather than later. 'Get your clothes together and get out!'

Blankly he looked at her, then a smile passed over his lips. 'In this weather? You must be joking.'

'Do I look like I'm joking?'

'You look like a clown, if that's any use.'

'Just get out. And take your pathetic youth-club jokes with you.'

The laughter served only to infuriate her further. Akimbo, statuesque, features of granite, she demanded: 'are you going to clear off? Out of my home and out of my life!'

Still laughing he collected the packet of cigarettes from the coffee table, casually lit one, then flicked ash onto the floor. 'Seeing how you never stop going on about housework, tidy that up.'

'Bastard.'

'All you ever talk about is tidying up. Housework Monday, window-cleaning Tuesday, you're driving me crazy. Has anyone told you that you're a bore?'

'Has anyone ever told you you're a nasty, arrogant, conceited little animal? If it wasn't for me playing mummsie half of the time you'd stink like an animal too. There's more man in a Beecham's powder. And you can sweep that ash up.'

'Pigs'll fly before I sweep that up.'

In bratty tones she mimicked him, 'pigs'll fly...You're so childish it's unbelievable. You could do to get a life.'

'Life? What do you know about life? There's more to living than having a so-called ideal home. You exist - that's all you do - you don't live. Anyone would think we were trapped in a detergent advertisement.'

'Wrong! Most people would think we were stuck in a pigsty. Or they would if they ever saw you loose in the home. Talk of pigs flying, they'd fly in the opposite direction if they caught a whiff of Little Lord Muck living on his own.'

Once they started there was no way of telling when it would stop.

'Do you expect me to walk around, every waking hour, worrying whether the dishes are washed or if the frigging carpets are spick and span?'

'The carpets you ruined with your cigs when you were drunk last night.'

'Oh, it's always me, isn't it? I'm always the guilty one. I don't suppose it's crossed your tiny little mind that you might have accidentally done it? You also smoke and you were just as drunk as I was.'

'That's it, blame me.'

'Well, you're blaming me, aren't you?'

'That's because you did it.'

'How can you be sure? How do you know for certain?'

'Because I do.'

'It was you who was sat there, where the burns are, by the gas fire. You said you were freezing when we came in. I was sat here, as always - are there any burns here? No!'

'You know everything, don't you?'

'Yes, that's the difference between us. You think you know and I do know.'

'I know you're full of shit.'

'Hark at Perfect Penelope - the girl who's never put a foot wrong in her whole life.'

'Oh, I don't think that, most definitely don't think that. If I'd never put a foot wrong I wouldn't have lived with you for the past year. You're the most worthless thing on two legs I've ever come across. It takes you all your time to change a light bulb.'

'Think you're bright do you? How come I have to change the vacuum bag every time it gets full?'

'I can do it. I just like seeing you get off your fat arse every now and then.'

'Bull. You just think you were put on earth to nag me, that's your problem. Well, I've news for you, I've some complaints of my own.'

'I don't care what you say, I want you out!'

'Oh, I thought it would be different now, now the boot's on the other foot.'

'Out!' She screamed as she left the room once more. Only this time to stomp up the stairs. From the landing she bawled: 'I'll have your bags packed in half-an-hour, phone a taxi to take you wherever you're going to stay.'

He made no effort to reply; instead blew smoke rings, watched - with little real interest - the downpour outside drip-drop-splash from branches and grey rooftops. Next door's moggie scrambled away along the top of the fence, presumably heading somewhere secretive, known to be dry. The neighbours were out then: at least they wouldn't be hearing any of this.

Incensed, wrathful, she rummaged through the chest of drawers, separating his clothes from hers, slinging socks, shirts and whatever into the suitcase she had just dragged from the spare room.

Until now he believed he had controlled his temper reasonably well. But now - now he could hear her packing - rage welled inside him. Irascibly, like a startled savage he sprang from the chair, bounded to the bottom of the stairs. 'Leave my fucking things alone! In weather like this do you think I'm going anywhere? If you're so keen to see the back of me piss off to your mother's for a few days.'

Her footsteps pounded across the ceiling. She glared over the banister, long hair hanging over eyes, nose and mouth. Briefly, this image stunned him - until her voice stung him back to life: 'and leave you to make an even bigger tip of my home, no chance. You're leaving and you're leaving today! I want you out. How many times do I have to tell you? Your lazy ways ruin everything I ever buy.'

'Oh, for frig's sake, it's only a carpet. We can get another, a new one.'

'The carpets are all but new anyway - you've no respect for anything of mine.'

'You don't deserve respect.'

'What was that?'

'I said you don't deserve respect. The way you were all over that poseur in the pub last night. One drink and you're bloody anybody's.'

'What are you talking about?'

'Don't come the innocent with me.'

'You talk absolute rubbish.'

'I do, do I?' He raced up the stairs, slipping and banging his knee as he did so. The dull pain aggravated anger. He and she came face to face, do-or-die, adversaries about to duel. 'If I hadn't been out with you you'd have been back at his place, no questions asked. How stupid do you think I am?'

'Stupid enough to make an idiotic accusation like that. And if it was true, which it isn't, it'd god damn make a change to you eyeing up anything in a skirt.'

'That's complete jealous nonsense.'

'And what you're saying isn't?' She pushed him in the chest.

'No!' The pungency of denial made her shudder. 'I could tell you wanted to sleep with him that...that...that shit dressed as a shop dummy.'

'He was better dressed than you.'

'He's a smarmy greasy fashion victim, that's all. And what's so insulting is that you made your intentions obvious right under my nose. Like a cheap tart. I'm surprised you don't wear white stilettos.'

She raised her hand. The palm wavered, held back, shackled by some invisible force: however much she wanted she felt unable to unleash the blow. For the time being.

'You...just...dare.' Temptation that was also a threat.

'And what? What will you do? Beat me like some sad cowardly excuse for a man. The sad excuse that you are.'

'If you strike me I'll do more than beat you - I'll fucking strangle you!' She fled to the bedroom in floods of tears. Before he could follow she had wedged the door tight, using the back of a chair

185

against the handle as security. 'I always knew you were a bastard,' she sobbed.

F-f-f-f-frustration demanded an outlet: he kicked the wall: a sizeable clump of plaster crumbled to the carpet. Fuck it. Fuck this house.

Downstairs he turned on the radio to drown the bitter torrent of tears and words: he made no attempt to find another station even though he detested the song currently on air. Feeling drained, defeatist, he collapsed into the armchair and sparked another cigarette. Perhaps he should give her something else to complain about and burn a hole in the cushion, that would show her. But on second thoughts he knew better - the whole in the wall was enough.

He removed his shoes. He wasn't going anywhere.

Upstairs sorrow flowed into spite. She got out her manicure set and with nail scissors vengefully cut random patterns in two of his favourite shirts. This act completed she scowled, cold, recklessly satisfied. Something had been achieved.

The radio continued to churn out hits that he did not care for. With speed or numb sluggishness - neither he nor she were sure - time passed. Eventually he heard the bedroom door open and the suitcase dragging on the floor. The suitcase thudded and bumped as it descended the flight of steps.

Though she had stopped crying her eyes were still puffed and red. He felt a twinge of guilt. 'I want you out.' Though determined her voice was now cool. He looked up at the ceiling, out of the window. 'I said, I want you out.'

'I heard you.' His voice had also lost its edge.

She waited for some move. Time stood still. They heard the local news bulletin. Four people had died in a terrible car accident. Retailers all across the region had reported a fall in sales. There were still no goals in the local derby. The rain was in for the weekend.

'Will you please get out?'

'No.'

She wanted - needed - to do something to gain the upper hand. His words always seemed to sting more than hers. Far too slowly she reached over to pick up the packet of cigarettes. Far, far too slowly. His hand shot out and claimed the packet. 'You've a nerve. Blame me for burning the carpet, threaten to throw me out because of it and then you want to smoke my cigarettes.' The irony was too much, he could not prevent himself smiling.

'You're not listening to my radio then.' She pulled the plug. She also could not resist the temptation to smile.

Together they considered the absurdity of the situation. It wasn't for the first time. 'Is the argument officially over?'

'I suppose so,' she sighed, relieved. They knew they had to stop doing this. For whatever reason the accursed circle seemed impossible to break. This did not appear to be a thing in their own hands any longer. They resembled infants forgiven - finally - for some misdemeanour that had been committed with full knowledge of the implications. Something avoidable yet strangely alluring. Like crayoning on wallpaper.

'I'll put the kettle on, then. Before I do, I've a confession to make - I got so angry I kicked some plaster out of the wall. It's all right, it'll be easy to fix. Whatever you might say I'm at least capable of doing that. And there's still some paint in the garage to touch-up with. I'll get to work as soon as we've had the cuppa...and a cuddle.'

'Oh.'

'You're not mad?'

'Well,' she squirmed, 'I've a confession, too.'

'What?'

'You made me so mad I've cut up your blue and your red and blue shirts.'

The information slowly sank in. 'You'd fucking better not have...'

Hell's bells, here we go again. She wished they'd stayed in bed that morning...

187

Supermarket

Later, the lights have dimmed. The workers and the customers have all gone their separate yet similar ways. Middle-aged to microwave meals, the soporific flicker of a screen, partners with their feet on the arms of the sofa. Perhaps some will call on neighbours, potter in the garage or enjoy a drink at the local. Romance is a fleeting thing. Romance is for those in the celebratory bloom of youth.

And those in the celebratory bloom of youth. They are high with that equally fleeting feeling of liberty: anything seems possible right now, and right now spans forever and eternal. Getting groomed, grooved and going. Drinking, drugs, clubs and cinemas. Whatever those with youth do away from the universally disapproving eye of ex-guardians; parents demoted to mere hoteliers.

And another watchful eye, that of a security camera, restlessly scans from left to right from right to left. Investigating desertion. Now the place is just a storeroom. A warehouse. A giant's pantry perhaps imaginative little Tommy Burns would say when he finally bored of his alien game. Tins. Hundreds and thousands of tins. An electrical hum from the frozen food area throbs through the emptiness.

Tomorrow is big money bonanza. Saturday. The weekend starts here. Long live the weekend. Hangovers, arguments, kids underfoot and cashback parking. Bungalows, bedsits, flats and households of hungry mouths to be fed. Everyone will forgetfully omit something from their list. The Almighty decrees it. It's one of Sod's laws.

The big day begins around 5:30am, when cleaners punctually or otherwise arrive. Joe Murphy - a rugged lifelong factotum with long flowing snowy locks and beard that endow him the appearance of a keep-fit Santa in casual attire - stands by the entrance, his deep gruff voice booming in the early fume-free air. Good morning and how are you to all. On his first day of employment with the supermarket, nearly two years ago to the day, jolly Joe was distressed to depression by the sleep deprived dearth of camaraderie and surplus of grumbles and groans amongst his workmates. So much so that by the end of that first shift the man who had spent his entire working life doing the menial jobs that no-one else wanted, pledged, hand on heart, that the early morning misery would never show its face again. At least while he was around.

Mopping lino floors has never been the same. Joe is a karaoke machine, a stand-up comedian and a fountain of obscure trivia rolled into one endearing chunk. The clan of cleaners, mainly middle aged women, almost enjoy hearing their alarms wail at the crack of dawn. Though the fun would come to an abrupt and short-tempered end if Derek Saddleby ever caught Joe dancing down the aisles, using the handle of a sweeping brush as a microphone, howling 'Be-Bop-A-Lula!'

'Comical and sort of educated,' Sylvia Bennett, one of the cleaning crew, describes Joe to her bingo partners. The bingo partners suspect that Sylvia, a widow for the best part of five years, has a crush on Joe. Even amongst the pungent fumes of disinfectant, it's always in the air. Small wonder it sells.

But all that be tomorrow. In the Friday teatime drizzle outside, Jennifer Addison waits beneath an umbrella for the No. 136 service to take her home. A couple of hours after the seedy scene in his office sex-pest Saddleby groped Jennifer in the rest room. Rearranging the rota he had ensured that her afternoon break did not coincide with anyone else's. Her breasts and hips feel filthy. Jennifer longs for a bath. Of the supermarket she has had enough. She will not return.

With dread Jennifer imagines the disappointment on Simon's face when she tells him that their plans are to be put on hold. She hopes her boyfriend will understand, take it the right way. She hopes he doesn't think there is anyone else. She dare not tell Simon the truth.

Jennifer knows she has one hope. The reason for her throwing a sickie on Monday. Were her parents right? Had she wasted Simon's money?

And the bastard Saddleby. What would happen if she reported that mucky greasy toad? Would people believe her? Or would people believe that she'd led him on? Some people, Jennifer knew, took one look at her and their minds were made up. People had always judged her by her looks. People like Saddleby.

As Jennifer steps forward and peers down the road to check whether her bus will be on time, a car pulls up behind her. Without looking the young woman knows who or rather what it is. 'Hello gorgeous, fancy a lift?' Jennifer turns, bends over, peers through the open car window. She doesn't smile or speak, just looks; stone-faced into the brown dead eyes of the manager. And then she spits. A whole grisly gobful. 'Kerb crawling is for red-light districts.' Jennifer quickly spins away and walks, never looking back. Walks. Just walks. Her head held high beneath the umbrella. Marching on and onwards. Homeward bound. Past the shops, offices, town hall, through the cheerless rainy streets of her hometown.

At the end of his working week Simon spends a few hours in the pub with his pals. He won't be home until nine-ish. A lonely few hours ahead. Jennifer was looking forward to tomorrow. Together they were to enjoy a buffet Chinese meal, inexpensive but tasty. Now, perhaps not...every last penny will have to be accounted for.

Jennifer shakes the weather from her brolly, turns the key in the lock and opens the front door. Immediately she spies the embossed envelope amid the jumble of mail shots from banks, fast food takeaways and supermarkets. She feels her heart jump. For thirty seconds she is dead weight, rooted to the spot, disabled by nervous anticipation. All hope will either be destroyed or realised by the contents of the envelope. This is the reason she threw a sick day on Monday.

Jennifer pulls herself together, summons courage and tears open the correspondence like a child with the wrapping of the biggest present on the pile.

'Dear Miss Addison' the letter begins. 'We are pleased...' Relief turns into joy. In the mirror at the bottom of the stairs even Jennifer is taken aback by the vitality of her smile. Catalogue models are paid handsomely, the pretty price of the portfolio now justified.

On the answering machine there is a midmorning message of congratulations from the photographer on Jennifer's first assignment. The girl cannot wait to break the good news to Simon.

No more Saddleby.

Though bikini clad cardboard cut-outs do present the latest got-to-have goods. Full circle, perhaps Jennifer will not have entirely left the supermarket behind.

The End

Now that she had done it - actually uttered those final fatal words - there could be no doubt. Her relief was proof of her conviction: it was over. The end. And all that remained was good-bye, get out, walk away. Get out - walk away; the words she repeated over and over, demanding then commanding...in vain. She didn't feel able: she was trapped. Some need to explain - be thought better of - held her back. 'Really, I still care for you but...things just don't seem to have been working out. For weeks I've known, deep down, that it' - she paused, corrected herself - 'we were over. Maybe longer than weeks, I've...' Her voice withered, could not survive the brooding chill of his silence. Words were useless. Only one thing. Get out - walk away.

But still she remained seated.

And he remained perfectly still. Knuckles white on the steering wheel, glazed eyes staring inexpressively ahead. Seeing but yet blind. Nothing beyond the breath-misted glass of the windscreen. Nothing beyond the tip of his nose.

She hadn't been sure how he would take the news. His reaction - or lack of - inspired pity but not much else. And that confirmed everything. She was doing the right thing.

But something else needed to be done. Something other than the right thing. But what? For want of anything better she wiped the windscreen clear with a tissue, carefully stuffed the damp waste into a redundant ashtray. He made no response, perhaps as unable as she felt unable to leave.

'I don't want to hurt you.'

Nothing.

This should really be only a matter of seconds. It should be easy. Make the decision and move. Out, get out and into the street. Instead she glanced sideways, nervously assessing the vacant profile beside her. And then she looked ahead. She just looked.

Had the street ever appeared so dreary as it appeared right now? Perhaps she'd never had time or reason to look so closely before. Look closely, at dull rows of nineteen-twenties terraces their humble facades scuffed by decades and weather. She supposed it would be apt if rain now fell; but the heavens were as dry of tears as her eyes.

Not a hundred yards away vague shadows tangled and smooched in a similarly parked car. Young and in love - or simple plain lust. That would be Susan White and her latest judging by the proximity of the other car to the parental White's front door. Once-upon-a-short-while-ago things would not have been so different in this car, though the couple inside were hardly teenagers. She pictured herself commenting, rather tangentially, on the full moon floating high above the primary school at the end of the road; next offering, coffee; instant-and-two-sugars ultimately leading to bed. But tonight, tonight was the end. All such ceremony had been resigned to the past, however fresh to mind.

Get out - walk away. And in mere minutes any vestige of uncertainty would be gone, banished, for all time. Until the next time. The next time with someone else.

No-one seemed right for her. It always ended like this.

She released the seat belt, slowly reached for the door handle. A prisoner attempting to outsmart an inattentive guard. The prisoner failed. 'Did you enjoy the film?' His voice a mechanical grating, a tone in which she had never heard him speak.

'I wasn't really taking it in, I had...other things on my mind.'

'Three out of ten. It was abysmal.'

'Oh.' Her hand made contact with the handle.

'Who is he?' Syllables like gears grinding.

The fingers stalled.

'There isn't an he.'

'When did you meet him? How long has it been going on behind my back?' A glower that lasted perhaps two seconds. Then he was staring at non-existence down the street or the imaginary barrel again.

Don't dally, life and limb move on, it was over. She pulled at the handle - no - reluctantly hesitated. Over...but not quite yet. Placing one hand to either cheek she apologised, 'I'm really sorry, Ian. Really truly sorry. You and me...you're not the one I need.' She never understood why she always apologised. Why should she feel as if she was doing something wrong? 'And who is he, the one you need, the one you've found?'

'I haven't found anyone,' she insisted.

The colour had drained from his face, now ghost-white in the poor light. 'I don't get it...I thought...we were good together. Think of the good times...and how many bad? Didn't...we have something special, a future?' Meaning to speak from the heart his words stuttered from tongue, resembling nothing so much as impersonal cliches uttered to anyone or no-one in particular. Certainly not the love of his life.

'I've work in the morning, I've got to be getting to bed.'

A dull thud - head striking the solid rim of the driver's wheel. 'Don't do this to me, Louise. Please.'

'Ian, I'm so sorry, but it's over.'

'Why?' His voice cracked. He coughed, cleared his throat. 'Why? Why? Why?' Each question accentuated by brow crashing sickeningly against wheel.

'Don't do this to yourself. We survive these things, Ian.'

His pain brushed aside the gentle touch that had reached out to him.

'No.' Thud. 'No.' Thud. 'No.'

The violence was uncharacteristic and alarming.

'I've got to go.'

The door opened but a fraction before he pounced; hand on hand, flesh a manacle to flesh. 'At least explain.'

'I've tried to explain.'

'Not enough.' His grip tightened.

'Ian, you're hurting...let go, you're scaring me.'

'Do you care if you hurt me?' Nevertheless he released her wrist, slightly. Ever so. 'Why?'

'I don't know if there is an explanation. Not one you could properly understand. I'm not sure myself...except to say that I know I feel nothing for you anymore. Nothing like I should feel, anyway.'

He let go. She kissed the red imprint on her wrist, mothering her own injury. Tomorrow there would be a bruise, perhaps.

'And that's it? Over. Gone. As cold - as black and white - as that? As if we never meant a thing.'

'I'm sorry, but that's it. Truly it. Over.' Too cruel to be real, to be really her, he thought. There must be something he could say:

'I'll change.' A vapid shot in the dark: too watery-weak to have passion: to be anyone she needed. Everything was decided.

'I don't want you to change.'

'What do you want?'

'I don't know.'

'Well, think.'

'I want to stop seeing you.'

How could he stop this? Prevent a terrible error.

'Whatever it is that's wrong, we can work on it, work it out.'

'We couldn't, we're beyond that.'

'I'll do anything.'

'There's nothing you can do.'

'I'll move in - or we'll buy a house - living together, that will smooth things over.'

'Ian, it's over.'

'One day, we could be happily married.'

'Ian, it's over.'

'Will you marry me?'

'It's over.'

'Say you will.'

'It's over! Finished!' Curt and damning and inevitable.

From shock through sorrow, despondency to anger; that other inevitable. 'What is it? Has he more money? A better car? A nice house?'

'There's no-one else. It isn't like that.'

'What is it, then?'

'How I feel.'

200

'Feel? Feel?'

'Yes, how I feel.'

'About who?' With a rush of blood he seized the collar of her jacket, ragged her fiercely: 'Who? Who? Tell me!'

'Ian...Stop it! Let me go! You'll...'

But only the sound of skull against window persuaded him to stop.

'Bully,' she groaned through the pain. 'I'm sorry Louise, so sorry. But I don't want to be without you. I'll do anything. Anything.'

'And that's your way of showing it. Get lost.'

She rub-nursed the small swelling to scalp.

'Please don't tell me there's someone else.'

It was an opportunity to avenge the pain. 'There is, if you really must know. I've slept with three other men in the last month alone,' she lied. 'Sleeping with you does nothing for me.'

'I knew it.'

He collapsed into the steering again. 'I could always tell that I was never enough, it was obvious from the word go - from the very start.'

'How do you mean?' Her discomfort had soon peaked, ebbed to a blunt throb; given way to bewilderment following Ian's devastated admission.

'When we were out together, other men and you, I always suspected that you...'

'Don't be ridiculous.'

'You were too good for me.'

'Now you're being pathetic.'

'It's always like this, in the end.' He was practically sobbing.

More than the fury of a moment before this display of vulnerability she found disquieting, embarrassing even. As though he should be ashamed.

Looking away Louise brusquely intoned, 'look, I must be going.' And she knew that she should have gone straight away, words really were useless.

'Going to him? Is he there, in the house?'

'I'll be alone. He doesn't exist, except in your insecurity.'

'Insecurity? There's reason to be, isn't there?'

'I haven't been happy, that's all there is to it.' Her formal, matter-of-fact tones stunned further: Louise was a virtual stranger. 'But I'm not the sort of person to go behind your back. I'd sooner have everything out in the open. Feel free to believe what you will.'

It would be pointless to listen to any more: she would listen to no more. Why had he not seen this coming? There must have been warnings. Humiliated, crestfallen, he did not try to detain her.

Having poured herself a glass of wine Louise sank back into the sofa, determined to relax - and be thankful a true course had irrevocably run. She knew she would not be persuaded to change her mind.

Why had it been necessary to break free of Ian? The very fact that she herself struggled to come to terms with the decision to split only served to further confound and confuse. Ian had never done her wrong and she had more than just liked him in the beginning. What was it - within her - that had changed? The head can't explain heart, vice versa: and that was the best she could offer. But no mistake, a burden had definitely lifted. It felt right.

Comfortable, outstretched, she refused to stir when the phone rang. The red light of the answering machine flickered, a click...'Hello. I am unable to take your call right now. Please leave your message and a contact number...' Louise's pre-recorded voice politely informed and requested.

'Louise, it's me. Talk to me. I want you to know I love you, this - this shouldn't be happening. Please don't finish this way. Pick up the phone, please. We need to talk.' Silence. The message was over. Ditto the relationship. This was the end. Peace.

She sipped at the wine.

Peace? There had always been peace. Many folk had considered them to be a perfect couple - they'd rarely argued, had each allowed the other freedom to come and do as they pleased. Definitely the sort of pairing lots of people would give...The week in Tunisia had been a horrible sham. But Ian couldn't be blamed for a squalid insect infested hotel. She had chosen the bloody place, booked the sodding holiday. He had wanted to go to Spain. But.

Did the holiday have anything to do with it? That would be just too bloody-minded and stupid. Is that where it started?

The phone again. 'Louise, will you talk to me? We've got to sort this out. I don't know what you've got into your head. It's no good pretending...' Speechlessness. Some indistinguishable background noise. End of message.

Pretending what?

The whole world might well have gone to sleep, not even a hint of breeze to rustle the leaves of the tree to the back of the house. The wine was good. So good she poured another glass. And though the clock read bedtime and beyond she continued to drink; and with a greater thirst, gulps rather than sips. Another glass.

Generous, reliable, Ian had been lots of things. None of them bad. What else could he have done to keep her happy?

Another quick top-up before sleep.

Lovesickness tried again. 'Answer the fucking phone! Just answer the fucking phone! Now! Do it! I'll kill you! I'll kill him! I'll see you together, you better believe it. I'll fucking kill the both of you!' Slam!

The wine had numbed Louise's capacity to care. Tipsy, giddied somewhat, she slid off the sofa, reached over - 'goodnight, good-bye'. Removing receiver from hook she studied a nearby photograph on the unit. His face like any other face in any other crowd. She emptied her glass.

Already the mobile she had left on the bedside locker had received three new messages. She bothered with none.

Louise stood examining her nakedness in the mirror. Who else was there? Ian's plaintive demand seemed to echo around the room. She was only thirty, her reflection still youthful. Sexual. In time there would be someone else. Maybe only weeks.

She considered a final glass of wine, decided against the idea. Tonight it had been done: get the night over with. Finished. The end.

Into night-dress and between sheets. Light switch - out. Darkness. Alone but not lonely. Who else? And there was no-one...not anyone...eyes tight shut...the image of...she turned over.

Even to herself she'd been trying to deny it. She regarded herself neither the flirty or disloyal sort of girl. But the smiles the newcomer to the office had been flashing at her for the past fortnight. There was definitely an attraction. She wanted to be touched. Considered reaching over for the something in her drawer. But no, that wouldn't be right, not tonight.

And nothing would come of it, she told herself, it was only a silly effect of wine. The newcomer to the office was probably married.

She wondered whether Ian had started drinking, hoped he wouldn't do anything they might both regret. Was there any need to worry? No, Ian wasn't like that, she felt sure. No, Ian wasn't like that. And Louise smiled, she had the reassurance of the mobile close at hand, come what may.

She remembered the alarm for the morning at the last moment. She fumbled to set it and - click - darkness fell again.

Soon Louise was sleeping.

Until The Sun Goes Down

And that August sun without love hate nor any emotion between continued to blaze down from the pure azure sky. Like the birds and bees the people instinctively understood that Mother Nature - that most whimsical matriarch of all - seldom casts aside her inhibitions and doubts and so extravagantly bestows all her children below such a precious gift. Such a blessed and glorious afternoon as this. Close your eyes close your ears and surely this was not England but some faraway, more exotic land.

Throughout parks and public gardens a parade of pretty young things. Brightly, scantily clothed, flaunting voluptuous flesh before ever attentive admirers. Those shirtless, tattooed youths who idle, siesta happy, on graffiti carved benches. Desiring the attainable, coveting the not-so - praying that Lady Luck, like the great daystar above, also scintillates, weaves magic of summer romance.

In streets between rows of terraces mischievous urchins crack and fry eggs on piping car bonnets; they hurl water-bombs, aim spurting pistols. While housewives abandon housework to bathe on beach towels carefully spread over recently trimmed lawns. Everywhere the fuzzed strains of radio stations broadcasting the latest reports, hits and useless titbits to each outlet turned on, tuned in.

On deck-chairs, outside 84 Sycamore Avenue, rest two old men, wistfully smiling as they enjoy perhaps the last of their many summers.

'This weather is as good as it ever got during the good old days, Sam, huh?'

Sam looked up into the yonder and smiled. 'George, I do believe you're right,' he replies, but only after some deliberation. In surprise George strokes palm over bald pate: he could hardly believe he had heard his friend utter such an admission. Like many an octogenarian Sam Brown found it difficult - almost impossible - to credit any good to these times being. Now that Sam actually had done so today could certainly be regarded as special, an honoured occasion. With a hearty smacking of lips George savoured the taste of a full glass of bitter. He replaced the glass on the small table that was between the two old friends and their seats.

'And we've seen some good days, some very good days. Some bad, but some very good days nevertheless,' Sam, after another lengthy period of consideration, expands.

George nods absolute agreement.

'We've seen a lot, seen a hell of a lot.' Still pondering, Sam scratches brow.

'Survived a hell of a lot, too.'

'Damn yes, our time was a crazy time. The Great Depression, Churchill and Hitler, The Cold War. There was always some -ism stirring up muck.'

'Aye, that's right, there was always some sort of calamity in the making. Tighten your belts for this crisis and that crisis - bloody Cuban missile crisis. Recession and boom and recession, one strike and another...'

'In our time there have been enough power mad lunatics to fill ten asylums...'

'Parliaments, the asylums are called,' George sagely interrupts.

'...Thatcher and Reagan. All the Saddams, Ayatollahs, Maos, Pol Pots...'

'Piss-pots and piss-potical ideas.'

'...Enough antichrists to fill hell.'

'Yes, a lot of hate, but you have to admit we've seen a lot of love as well.'

'Never a truer word, George my lad. And good men can never be kept down, no. Because here we still are, sipping beer and enjoying a fine summer's day. More stamina than the lot of it and them put together.' Both old-timers laugh heartily at the idea. Then melancholically, as an afterthought, as if their mirth had in some way been disrespectful, Sam went on to propose: 'some good men did go down though.'

'Our Alec, your Frank. That bloody war.'

'Good boys, a waste of fine young men. It's been often said, but a waste of fine young men all the same.'

'We were the lucky ones, went down the pit. Mind, the pits were almost as dangerous in those days.'

'I remember Tom Rodgers, had a leg amputated after a landslide. Had to talk to him, try to keep his mind off the pain while medical help arrived. In terrible agony the poor fellow was.'

'Bert Mills, they never had a chance to get help to him. Buried alive under four ton of filthy black stuff. Six kids he had to support...left behind.'

The deck-chairs creak as George and Sam recline, solemnly reflecting a working life underground. George had always attributed his own relative good fortune and health to the discovery of a fossilised snail-like creature down Sharlston Colliery when he was a young man of nineteen. The very moment he had held the relic between thumb and forefinger he had ascribed to it talismanic qualities. The fossil had been safely preserved to this present day, an ornament on the mantelpiece beside the picture of Emma, his wife, as she was then, a rose of youth, all those long agoes since. George had always intended to have his archaeological find identified by whichever expert it is that identifies such things, but he had never got round to it.

This weather was really out of the ordinary. With his hand George fanned his face. Sam sighed peacefully.

While elsewhere - that clockwork mayhem - the grand order of things, struggles on. Sunburnt and exhausted road workers jig with pneumatic drills sending the only clouds to be seen - those of dust - drift-dancing into a vacant bus shelter. The hottest day for a decade the forecasters had predicted and who could disagree? Office staff loosen stifling ties and collars, van drivers microwave behind windscreens, factory workers suffer a shop-floor sauna, the deafening decibels of industrial machinery drowning their mutterings of dissent.

Across the town centre a blind man's guide panted heavily. Amid prams and trolleys, wherever the refuge of shade could be found, the hound paved a route. Infants under peaked hats follow the dog's trail with wide-eyed interest, slurping noisily on ice lollies all the while. Mothers purchase family necessities and market day bargains from stall holders swooning in the hot toil of service. The traders swear that this be some gargantuan sacrifice; a hefty price to pay to gain a honest profit.

Almost everyone wanted to be home.

And old George sat beside Sam in the garden at home, listened, a little dreamily, to the sounds of suburbia. The old fellow had had get-up-and-go kids for sure, had always owned a radio, then a television set...But a car, like those vroom-vrooming away in the background, he had never wanted one. George had never much wanted anything except happiness. And despite the trials of over three-quarters of a century he reckoned he had achieved that, in the main. Though it was one of the bitter-sad facts of later life that the people he had shared his happiness with had passed on by now. Wife, parents, brothers, sisters, friends - and a few enemies too - remains in the cemetery, yet still alive in memory. As George took another sip of beer they returned, the faces the places from down the years. It seemed so clear, as if his four score and more had in fact been one long continuous yesterday. Of the details nothing appeared to have been forgotten...

Chalked pavement games and street-gang cricket on the green. The foolish drunken scraps and scrapes of adolescence. The close-knit camaraderie of those born heir to nothing but an head-lantern and pickaxe. He recalled shy awkward crushes and the first kiss with his childhood sweetheart, later wife. The only one for him, ever. George could hear the sing-song happy church-bells of matrimony and see, like he could see the palm of his hand should he raise it, the proud congratulatory smiles all around. And then the old man was palpably touched, turned sombre, by the slow cortege and the tears of their beautiful daughters.

Chronology vanished, back further again. There was a clergyman's sanctimonious scolding for the sin of stealing apples from a vicarage orchard. Sam, Frank, Alec and he red-handed and red-faced. Laughter.

Conker gathering, snowballing and sledding, and how there wasn't a single white Christmas anymore.

George could nigh taste the sandwich his mother had carefully, lovingly prepared for his first shift: and that pint of stout his father handed over when he returned home later that day. The birth of babies June and Marilyn. Wetting the twins' heads had culminated in a night in Castleford's cells. George had never been able to remember exactly what he had done. The police turfed him into the starry early hours without explanation or reprise. Then a little later, Keith had come into the world.

Bank Holiday donkey rides with the bairns in Blackpool. Windy wet weeks in Scarborough and Brid. He'd always liked that pub, the one by the pier.

There was the time Jimmy Harris and he were caught selling knocked-off bottles of pop and perfume, cheap and by the truckload - the bottles had fallen from the back of the proverbial lorry after all, or so they had guilelessly claimed. The miscreant pair had been fined, a fair sum back then, two whole weeks wages.

Poor Jimmy Harris. He had been killed in a road accident. Leaving 'The Fox' after downing his customary Friday gallon Jimmy had staggered and lurched, back and forth, finishing, ending all, beneath the wheels of a speeding vehicle. The community had said, jokingly, to ease the pain of the passing of one of its most famous and well-liked characters, that it had been the same lorry that all Jimmy's cut-price wares had conveniently fallen from.

Yes, all the names, the places, and some of the dates. George even knew, without a flicker of doubt, where and with whom he had been when news came through that Mr Armstrong had made his giant leap for mankind. Hardly anyone in the club had believed it, thought it some sort of conspiracy theory. And look at how technology had come on since!

Oh, they were the days. Sam, with his everyday mourning and mulling, was right. *They really were the days.*

And Sam, characteristically, was also travelling through time; his watery gaze distracted, set on nothing. Nothing here, nothing now, least ways. 'For whatever reason,' Sam reminisced, speaking his thoughts aloud rather than initiating conversation, 'I can always picture us playing in the fields with Alec and Frank - there's a big bloody estate been built over the fields now. We were throwing a stick so Alec's - your - dog would fetch it.'

'Molly the dog was called.'

'And Frank fell into the stream, head over heels, bloody saturated he was. Mind the water was clean in the streams back then, not like all this pollution you get nowadays.'

'Shame for the kids, there's nowhere safe for them to play now.'

'We can't have been more than ten years old at the time. Frank had a fight with Alec for laughing too loudly.'

'Who won?'

'Frank. A bloody tearaway he was. Shame about the bomb that got him.'

'At our time of life, Sam, it's best to think about the good things.'

'Yes, at least all our kids grew up all right.'

'And the grandkids aren't doing too bad, so far.'

'All these bloody drugs worry me.'

'They shouldn't, things are out of our hands now. We've done our bit - and done it well.'

'Aye, maybe you're right. Nothing left for us to do except enjoy a drink on a grand sunny day like this.' Sam glanced at the glasses on the table.

'I often wonder - do you think He exists?' George asked.

'I don't bloody care whether He does or He doesn't. And if He does He'll get a right rollocking from me when I reach the pearly gates.'

George smiled. 'He deserves one, I'll say that. Tell me Sam, if you could turn the clock back would you change anything?'

'No, no regrets.'

'Me neither. I don't regret one single thing.'

The two old friends clinked their now almost empty glasses of beer. 'Cheers.'

And the sun that was older still continued to blaze.

Supermarket

Derek Saddleby straightens his tie before turning the handle of the unlocked door of Acacia Avenue. He has had to drive round the block five times to quash his anger at suffering the disgrace of having a mere check-out girl spit in his face. 'Hello darling,' Derek calls out affectionately, a gentle responsible husband and father. There is no reply. Uh-uh? Then Saddleby remembers and the puzzled expression disappears as quickly as it appeared. 'Tonight,' Derek told Deborah that morning over cornflakes and vitamin packed fruit-juice, 'I'll be home late. Unfortunate, I know, but some new workers have to be shown the ropes of stocktaking. Hopefully it won't take too long.' Saddleby had been optimistic. He was certain that he would be able to convince Jennifer Addison that sharing a motel bed with him, after the day's work was done, would be no bad thing.

Derek's ears strain on hearing a faint sound. The noise is coming from upstairs. It increases: 'uh-uh-uh-Uh-Uh-UH-UH-UH-OOOOOOHHHHHH!!!!' The unmistakable sound of ecstasy.

Derek Saddleby's knees go weak.

The Operatives

M S Green

A seventies child of West Yorkshire. Factotumesque, he has held posts in offices, as a marquee erector, shop assistant, and manual worker at various factories, amongst others. Enjoying a lengthy period unemployed in between. As ex-journeyman musician he has been drunk at - and played - the seedy venues of many major UK cities. During the mid-nineties he co-formed and promptly helped bankrupt a small independent record label. He penned a fast-selling Manchester based music fanzine around the same time. Currently works on *A Kind Of Living*, his first novel.
Supermarket, Going Back There, Junk Food Mash, Face Arranger, Genitalia, Carpet Burns, The End, Until The Sun Goes Down.

Alan Green

Heralded as the finest blues harmonica player in the West Riding - you can hear him fleetingly on *The Chapter* - he walks his own pace. A veteran of many a short term contract, he knows his way around the warehouse estate. A passionate researcher of local history, he is acknowledged as an authority on Knottingley's Wild West hero, Ben Thompson. A book on Thompson is an ongoing, long-term project. He has a daughter, Jessica, and lives in Pontefract.
Squelch, Dustbin Man, Kip

Clayton Devanny

A musician and songwriter, Clayton has been the lead guitarist for an assortment of bands, primarily playing blues and funk. He has composed and produced soundtracks for several websites, and a number of his articles on music have been published in the *route* newspaper. He currently plays guitar and sings for Budists, you can hear him on the *Warehouse* CD.
Urban Deprivation From The Palace of Wisdom, Limbo Land

Simon Nodder

After five years studying Art & Design and Film & TV Production, Simon spent four 'mind numbing' years as a warehouse operative on the Whitwood and Normanton Industrial Estate. He is currently studying to become a registered mental health nurse.

Inside The Devil's Lungs, Of Those Who Live in the Shadows

Jono Bell

An all-round versatile musician, he pushes himself to create the kind of music he likes to hear, rather than what he already knows. This has inspired him to experiment with dance grooves and soulful synthesised sound. He has played drums for a number of bands and was a founder member of Budists in 1999. You can hear his drumming on *Ain't That A Bitch*. His story *Survival Instinct* was told almost verbatim one night over a dinner table.

Survival Instinct

Warehouse CD

The Chapter

1. My Day (Intro)
2. She Far Out
3. Born
4. Morning
5. Round and Round
6. The Deliverance
- 7. My Day
8. Hometown Inevitability

Budists – Ain't That A Bitch!

9. Ain't That A Bitch
10. Song #1
11. Tarts Pants
12. Medicine Man
13. Scary-Go-Round (Trip By The C)
14. Soul Provider
15. Pank Funk
16. Hair Today
17. If We Try

The Chapter

This EP was written sat in the tall walled halls of purgatory…under time's great ticking clock…awaiting a decision from a soulless monkey…off the back of a long haul…spending precious time on the nightshift with an oil barrel gang from the back streets of nowhere…hunting weekend solace in a wasted tango with Stella Artois and a spliff or two…watching friends on a knife's edge dance the dance of the pin-eyed toothless zombie while, all the time I kept one eye on the front door…

Dean Smith - Lyrics & Vocals
David Stych - Guitars & Arrangements
Big Daddy Folk - Bass & Banjo
Rev Al Green - Harmonica
Princess Zara Gurtler - Cello
Steve Dymond – Piano, Fender Rhodes and Hammond Organ
Katy Harris – Clarinet
Ianto Thornver – Percussion

Production David Stych
Engineered Pat Grogan
Recorded Woodlands Studio, Castleford UK August 98

Thanks *to all of the above for their time and magical input. Cheers Browny, Devanny and Graham for those late nights with red wine carving out this material in the early days; The Mermaids, The Squirt and Mr South, can't forget crazy Pat Grogan and his cigarettes, Sime Bell and the then Buzzing Chairs for the loan of instruments; Chris Dunderdale and Lord Lathem, Sally Smith for the patience, my brother and sister in Holland, the late Richard Gale, Little Wayne, Lee and Monk, Stanley, Ryan and Red Eyed Mickwicker, Mexican Glen, The Martian, Fatha Gibbs, Col Bowkett, Bod, Carin Verbruggen for the original cover shots, Ian Daley and his seriously comic nature, and everyone else I forgot. Cheers.*

Budists - *Ain't That a Bitch!*

Written and arranged by Abraham/Bell/Devanny/Dymond.
Recorded live at Woodlands Studio, Castleford.
Engineered by Pat Grogan.
Tracks 2,3,5 & 7 recorded May 2000
Mixed by Pat Grogan.
Tracks 1,4,6,8 & 9 recorded July 2000
Mixed by Pat Grogan & Steve Dymond.

On these recordings;

Clayton Devanny - played guitar and sang.
Jono Bell - played drums.
Steven Dymond - played keyboards.
Robert Abraham - played bass and sang a little.

The Saxaphone on track 6 and Clarinet on track 9
was provided by Dale - nice one, blind boy.

*BUDISTS wish to thank everyone who was involved with
the inspiration and creation of this cd - you know who you are. To name but a
few; everyone at ROUTE and YAC - Ian D., Shigg Smith, Nicole Zep,
Slasher & Goll thankyou for your continuous support; Stressed Pat G. - the
unhappiest man in the world made us sound not bad; massive thankyou's to our
friends and loved ones for giving us drink and drugs or the money to acquire
such - AG/AW/JP/NR/HA/SJ and many, many more...cheers!*

This album is dedicated to those who enjoy it. Peace.

One Northern Soul - *J R Endeacott*
ISBN 1-901927 17 2

If that goal in Paris had been allowed then everything that followed could have been different. For young Stephen Bottomley something died that night. One Northern Soul follows the fortunes of this Leeds United fan as he comes of age in the dark days of the early eighties with no prospects, no guidance and to cap it all, his beloved football team suffer relegation to the Second Division.

This book is a reminder of a recent past and of connected fates. J R Endeacott has drawn a story that captures the mood of a time and a place, bottling the atmosphere of the terrace in its final days as disaster was about to strike and bring about wholesale and lasting change.

Kilo - *M Y Alam*
ISBN 1-901927 09 1

Khalil Khan was a good boy. He had a certain past and an equally certain future awaited until gangsters decided to turn his world upside down. They shattered his safe family life with baseball bats but that's just the beginning. They turned good, innocent and honest Khalil into someone else: Kilo, a much more unforgiving and determined piece of work. Kilo cuts his way through the underworld of Bradford street crime, but the closer he gets to the top of that game, the stronger the pull of his original values become. When he finally begins to rub shoulders with the men who inadvertently showed him the allure of crime, the more convinced he becomes that it is sometimes necessary to bad in order to achieve good.

'M Y Alam consistently articulates the experience of dual cultural identity, of being British born with Pakistani heritage and he violently runs this through the mixer with life on the mean streets seasoned with references to hip-hop and American gangster movies.'

The Blackstuff - *Val Cale*
ISBN 1-901927 14 8

'The mind is like a creamy pint of Guinness…The head is the engine that drives you through the day…the fuel however lies in the blackstuff, in the darkness, in the depths of the unexplored cave which is your subconscious mind…this is the story of my journey through the blackstuff.'

The Blackstuff is a true story of a road-trip that sees Val Cale in trouble in Japan, impaled in Nepal, ripped off at a vaginal freak show in Bangkok, nearly saturated by a masturbating Himalayan bear in the most southerly town of India and culminates in a mad tramp across the world looking for the ultimate blowjob and the meaning of life.

The Blackstuff is *not* just a book. It is *not* just the opinion of an individual who feels that he has something important to say. This is a story which every last one of us can relate to, a story about the incessant battle between our internal angels and our demented demons. This is an odyssey to the liquefied centre of the brain, a magic carpet ride surfing on grass and pills, seas of booze, and the enormous strength of the human soul.

The Blackstuff takes you beyond the beach, deeper into the ocean of darkness that is the pint of stout in your head…

Weatherman - *Anthony Cropper*
ISBN 1-901927 16 4

Ken sits out the back, in the flatlands that surround Old Goole, and watches the weather. That's what he was doing with poor Lucy, that fateful day, sat on the roof of his house, lifting her up to the sky. Lucy's friend, Florrie, she knew what would happen.

All this is picked up by Alfie de Losinge's machine, which he had designed to control the weather. Instead, amongst the tiny atoms of cloud formations, he receives fragmentary images of events that slowly unfold to reveal a tender, and ultimately tragic, love story.

In this beautifully crafted first novel, Anthony Cropper skilfully draws a picture of life inextricably linked to the environment, the elements, and the ever changing weather.

Very Acme - *Adrian Wilson*
ISBN: 1 901927 12 1 £6.95

New Nomad, nappy expert, small town man and ultimately a hologram – these are the life roles of Adrian Wilson, hero and author of this book, which when he began writing it, was to become the world's first novel about two and a half streets. He figured that all you ever needed to know could be discovered within a square mile of his room, an easy claim to make by a man who's family hadn't moved an inch in nearly seven centuries.

All this changes when a new job sends him all around the world, stories of Slaughter and the Dogs and Acme Terrace give way to Procter and Gamble and the Russian Mafia. He starts feeling nostalgic for the beginning of the book before he gets to the end.

Very Acme is two books within one, it is about small town life in the global age and trying to keep a sense of identity in a world of multi-corporations and information overload.

Like A Dog To Its Vomit - *Daithidh MacEochaidh*
ISBN: 1 901927 07 5 £6.95

Somewhere between the text, the intertext and the testosterone find Ron Smith, illiterate book lover, philosopher of non-thought and the head honcho's left-arm man. Watch Ron as he oversees the begging franchise on Gunnarsgate, shares a room with a mouse of the Lacota Sioux and makes love to Tracy back from the dead and still eager to get into his dungarees. There's a virgin giving birth under the stairs, putsch at the taxi rank and Kali, Goddess of Death, is calling. Only Arturo can sort it, but Arturo is travelling. In part two find out how to live in a sock and select sweets from a shop that time forgot and meet a no-holds barred state registered girlfriend. In part three, an author promises truth, but the author is dead - isn't she?

In this complex, stylish and downright dirty novel, Daithidh MacEochaidh belts through underclass underachieving, postponed-modern sacrilege and the more pungent bodily orifices.

**For the full list of route fiction and poetry titles
please visit www.route-online.com**

Route Subscription

Route's subscription scheme is the easiest way for readers to keep in touch with new work from the best of new writers. Subscribers receive a minimum of four books per year, which could take the form of a novel, an anthology of short stories, a novella, a poetry collection or mix and match titles. Any additional publications and future issues of the route paper will also be mailed direct to subscribers, as well as information on route events and digital projects.

Route constantly strives to promote the best in under represented voices, outside of the mainstream, and will give support to develop promising new talent. By subscribing to route, you too will be supporting these artists.

The fee is modest.

UK £15
Europe £20 (35€ approx)
Rest of World £25(US$40 approx)

Subscribe online now at www.route-online.com

To receive a postal subscription form email your details to books@route-online.com or send your details to:
route, school lane, glasshoughton, wf10 4qh, uk

Warehouse is a title on the route subscription scheme.